VERA'S VENTURE

World War II is over, but new problems confront Vera. Her wartime job ends, and her husband Geoff is invalided out of the army and needs work. With two young children they must leave their home and move into a rundown cottage in Norfolk. Geoff has taken an engineering job with the Fen River Board. And whilst the river banks desperately need strengthening, floods are threatening the flat Fenlands, and Vera must protect her family.

ANNE HOLMAN

VERA'S VENTURE

Complete and Unabridged

LINFORD
Leicester

First published in Great Britain in 2011

First Linford Edition
published 2012

British Library CIP Data

Holman, Anne, *1934 –*
    Vera's venture. - - (Linford romance library)
    1. Carter, Vera (Fictitious character)- -Fiction.
    2. Love stories. 3. Large type books.
    I. Title II. Series
    823.9′2–dc23

    ISBN 978–1–4448–1324–1

Published by
F. A. Thorpe (Publishing)
Anstey, Leicestershire

Set by Words & Graphics Ltd.
Anstey, Leicestershire
Printed and bound in Great Britain by
T. J. International Ltd., Padstow, Cornwall

1947

Vera Parkington felt a stab of disappointment when the midwife told her that her squalling newborn baby was a boy. 'I'd hoped for a daughter,' she said. But after the infant was placed in her arms she immediately fell in love with him.

Her husband, Geoff, was thrilled to have another boy and whispered in Vera's ear that she could have a girl next time.

Happy but exhausted, Vera smiled at him, before she went to sleep.

Now the war was over — but her worries weren't.

Her husband was still recovering from the mental trauma he'd suffered during the war. Geoff had been pensioned out of the army, but now he urgently needed a job. Although Geoff had been a high-ranking officer, it was of little value in post-war Britain because many ex-servicemen were seeking employment.

Vera had no job prospects, either. The British Restaurants were closing and with it her previous position as a supervisor. She couldn't possibly go back to work as a chef in a first class restaurant as she did before the war, because working during the evening hours would be impossible with two young children to look after.

Nursing her newborn baby, she felt blessed to have her family — but was feeling troubled as she anticipated what lay ahead for them.

★　★　★

Back home after the birth, Vera picked up the baby they had named Peter to wind him after a feed, murmuring sadly, 'Our family has another problem — we have to move out of this cottage very soon.'

The farm cottage they rented was

needed by the farmer to house a new farm worker and his family now that the Land Army girls had left the farm.

Vera had liked living in the cottage. But now — where could they go? Much as she loved her mother she didn't fancy living with her — and nor would her elderly mother and step-father appreciate having a young family plonked on them.

She was distracted by the sound of a car engine outside and, getting up, she walked to the window, looking out at the grey winter scene, and was delighted to see Margaret had come.

Miss Margaret Smallwood was one of her British Restaurant staff who had taken over her job as British Restaurant supervisor.

'Here you are,' said Margaret hauling in some surplus wartime pots and pans. 'I got them for next to nothing as they closed down the canteen, and I thought you'd find them useful when you move . . . '

Margaret was a very capable young woman — but bossy, too.

'Thanks,' Vera said, grateful for any help she could get.

'Let me hold the babe while you get me a cup of tea.'

Vera grinned. Trust Margaret to start ordering her about, but as Margaret had a child of her own she knew all about looking after babies.

'How's Deanna?' Vera called from the kitchen where she'd gone to make the tea as she'd been told to do.

'Starting school in September.'

Vera raised her eyebrows. How quickly the time had gone by! It seemed only yesterday that Deanna was as small as her new baby. 'I bet Deanna looks sweet in her school gym slip.'

'Oh, yes, she does — she doesn't want to take it off. Gone were the days when little girls liked pretty dresses.'

Vera brought in two mugs of tea saying, 'Well, the utility clothes in the shops for children aren't exactly pretty, are they? Wait till Deanna's a little older, and the wartime restrictions ease, then she'll love dressing like a princess.'

Margaret laid the sleeping baby into his Moses basket, and picked up her drink saying, 'Hmm! Those days of luxury we remembered before the war seem far away — and this year has started by becoming one of the coldest winters on record.'

That was undoubtedly true. It had been very cold in the country, with ice and snow adding to the difficulties caused by many after-the-war shortages.

'Things must get better soon,' said Vera, frowning, thinking they had survived the harsh war years and things couldn't get much worse.

Seeing Vera's expression, Margaret said brightly, 'Actually, I've come with an idea for you to chew over.'

'Oh, yes?'

Margaret's angular form sank into an armchair, she crossed her long legs and drank her tea. Then she smacked her lips and said triumphantly, 'I've found a new job!'

'Well done!' Vera said, albeit with a touch of envy.

'And one for you, Vera — if you want it.'

Vera blinked. 'How can I possibly go out to work with children to look after?'

'Well, I did. Deanna was sent to a baby-sitter.'

Vera knew that was true. Margaret was one of her original British Restaurant staff and having a baby to look after didn't stop her from learning to become her best cook and organiser.

Vera smiled. 'You are an exception, Margaret.'

'No, I'm not. Women are used to having to work during the war. Many now want to keep earning, so I can't see them all going back to their kitchen sink.'

Vera nodded. Some women would — and some wouldn't. 'But there aren't baby sitters in this part of the world.'

'Vera! Hear me out, will you ... ' Margaret put down her mug and wagged her finger at her friend.

Curious, Vera leaned forward to hear what Margaret had to offer.

'I'm going to be the county's School Meals Organiser,' said Margaret, proudly. Then she added, 'And you can work for me — if you'd like to?'

Stunned to think that she was to reverse her position as the boss to being under one of her raw recruits, Vera gulped. She was the expert Cordon Bleu chef — not Margaret. But did it matter? The school meals she remembered from her day were cold mince and tapioca pudding. Far removed from high-class restaurant menus.

'Crumbs!' muttered Vera.

'You'll be in charge of several school kitchens. Twenty-seven of them to be exact. And you can have a free lunch at one of them every day.'

'Oh, ta,' retorted Vera turning her back on her friend as she folded some nappies. She was doing her best not to show how disappointed she felt having to contemplate a job far below her capabilities.

Margaret huffed, 'Well, think about it. Has Geoff found a job yet?'

'No, he hasn't.'

'Any plans?'

'I don't know. He keeps trying.'

Margaret drained her tea cup. 'Well, I have a job possibility lined up for him, too.'

Margaret had known Geoff since they were children, and Geoff had found Margaret a job at the beginning of the war when she found herself pregnant and a widow.

He'd kindly fixed her up with a place to stay and a job at the British Restaurant, so now it seemed Margaret was trying to do the same for Geoff by assisting him to find work.

'What's the job?'

'Engineer in charge of flood defences.'

Vera perked up. At least it was an engineering job. Her Geoff was acknowledged as being a skilled engineer. But she said cautiously, 'You must remember he was injured during the war. He still isn't quite over the mental shock . . .

anyway, supposing he does like the idea, where will we live?'

'The job comes with a cottage.'

Vera was silent. Wondering.

Not for long, though, as her two dogs came bounding in followed by her three-year-old son, Victor, and Geoff, her good-looking husband, who'd been out walking the dogs.

'Hello, Margaret!' he called coming in and removing his cap and placing his walking stick in the umbrella holder.

He walked up to Margaret and bent to give her a quick kiss on the cheek. Then he kissed Vera and the baby.

'We're starving after our long walk,' he announced. 'And with two cooks in the house we expect something to eat. Don't we, Vic, my lad?'

Vic, who'd already snuggled on to Vera's lap, nodded.

Vera grinned. Finding food to eat was hard these days — cooking it was the easy part. Wartime dark-looking bread with a scraping of margarine, was all that came to mind.

Margaret came to the rescue. 'That reminds me, I made some brawn the other day. It's quite tasty, so I've brought you some in a basin.'

Vera sighed with relief. Brawn, like most scrag ends of meat was considered poor man's fare — like tripe and onions — but it was nutritious. Something for them to eat.

'Thanks,' Vera said, hoping Geoff would not turn his nose up at it. She'd tried giving him heart the other day and he'd become quite shirty about it. He'd apologised afterwards, but it made Vera aware that she would have to disguise the cheap cuts of meat so that the family didn't know the name of it.

However, Vera was a good cook and ingenious when it came to preparing food.

Margaret said she couldn't stay long and proceeded to tell Geoff about the job she'd heard about and thought might interest him, while Vera went into her kitchen to prepare something for them to eat.

Fighting with herself not to allow the problems she faced from making her feel depressed, Vera hummed the well-known wartime song, *Pack up your troubles in your old kit bag and smile, smile, smile.*

Indeed, she reminded herself, she had a lot to smile about, really. Her family were well. Although she had to embark on a new phase in her life — so had many people now that the war was over. Having to take a job, working under Margaret's direction, would do her no harm — other than her pride!

All she had to do was to embark on a new venture — which was exciting.

A little time later, she heard Geoff say to Margaret, 'Shall I tell her — or will you?'

'You explain everything to her, Geoff,' Margaret called out. 'I must dash. I'm running late.' Getting up she went into the kitchen and, quickly bidding Vera goodbye, she strode out of the cottage in a flash.

Vera knew there was no arguing with Margaret if she was determined to do something, so she went outside and waved her off.

Difficult Decisions

Vera was delighted to see the animated look on Geoff's face.

'I gather the job Margaret told you about was one that interests you?' she queried as she put a plate of food down on the table.

'Mmm,' he replied, seeming to be too hungry to talk about it as he examined his plateful of food. Then Vera was relieved when he began to eat it without questioning, or complaining, about the meat.

Bringing a small bowl of food for Vic, who was sitting in his high chair, she gave the child a pusher in one hand and a spoon in the other saying, 'Now eat it all up, like Dad.'

Vera was pleased to see them both tucking in. Preparing tasty and nutritious food from basic ingredients was a skill she'd acquired during wartime, and no-one did it better than her. The high-class cookery she'd been trained to do was a thing of the past.

'Well,' Vera said as they finished their meal, 'aren't you going to tell me about this job Margaret mentioned?'

'Oh, er, yes,' Geoff seemed to struggle to bring his mind back to talking about what Margaret had told him. 'It's a job I'm definitely interested in . . . '

'Well, that's a good start!'

Geoff looked at his wife, saying, 'Yes, it would be a challenge for me. And it would mean working and living in the Fenlands. Not a lot going on there, except farming and the wildlife.'

Exasperated, Vera asked, 'What *exactly* is this job?'

'Oh, the Fen river authorities are a bit worried about the river banks being able to cope with the high water levels, they need — '

'Engineers. Like you.'

Geoff grinned at his wife. 'They need to raise the river banks in places — to prevent flooding.'

'You can't do that!'

'Well, no, not without help. They are drafting in troops and prisoners-of-war to do the manual work — but they also need supervisors to tell the working men what to do — where the banks need strengthening and that sort of thing.'

Vera frowned. 'You don't know anything about that kind of work!'

Geoff got up from the table and went over to the range fire to use his penknife to scrape out the ash from his pipe. Then, as he took out his leather tobacco pouch to fill his pipe, which he put in his mouth, he took a spill and lit it.

Looking thoughtful as he lit his pipe, he said between puffs, 'That is true. It would be a new kind of work for me. I would have to learn — so I may not get the job even if I applied for it.'

Then Vera began to feel she should be encouraging, and as she began to fill the tray of dishes to be washed she said, 'Surely, that's their decision. They wouldn't give you the job if they didn't think you could do it.'

'That's not the only thing . . . '

Delaying taking the filled tray out into the kitchen, she looked puzzled.

He came over to her and said, 'We need somewhere to live now and the cottage that we could have is in a very remote area of the Fens. No buses.'

Vera gasped. With no car of her own — and Geoff would have his for his work — she would be very cut off.

'And the Fen people are a bit strange . . . '

'Oh?'

'Oh, don't get me wrong, they are as normal as anyone, but for centuries they've been living in rural areas far away from towns. They have their own way of saying things.'

Vera knew Geoff had knowledge of people living on the east coast because his wartime job had been an engineering project where he had to travel up and down the eastern side of England overseeing the work.

'Well, that's no worse than going to work abroad,' said Vera, determined not to allow her feelings about the disadvantages prevent Geoff from taking a job he was keen to do. She carried the tray of dishes to be washed into the scullery.

Geoff followed her. 'You may find it lonely, stuck in the middle of potato fields with two young children.'

Vera stood looking at him as the sink filled with hot water and she picked up the mop in her hand. 'I won't get bored, if that's what you mean — Margaret didn't tell you about *my job* then?'

As Geoff stared at her she wished she hadn't mentioned it. She hadn't meant to make his decision to go for his job more difficult.

Geoff was such a loveable man. Vera wanted to help him adjust to post-war life. So she shouldn't have mentioned any difficulty she might have taking up a new job herself — and it wouldn't be long before Vic needed to go to school.

Vic began to clamour and wanted to go and play, so Geoff released him from his high chair and lifted the boy down on to the ground, saying, 'Get your train set out while I'm helping Mum, and we'll play for a bit before bedtime.'

As the boy scampered off, Vera thought how wonderful it was her husband got on so well with Vic. Having a trusting little son, and non-critical dogs, too, had helped Geoff to overcome his war-injury emotional problems. He was still vulnerable — the doctor had warned her he could suffer a relapse.

While Vera continued with the washing up, Geoff got out the dog bowls and put a few scraps and biscuits in each as the two dogs sat and looked up expectantly at him. 'Actually, Margaret did mention that she could fix you up with a job,' he said.

Vera stopped splashing about in the washing-up water and listened.

Watching the dogs devour their food, Geoff remarked, 'Cooking school meals should be a doddle for you!'

Without bothering to wipe her hands, Vera turned and walking quickly over to him put her arms around his neck and kissed him.

'To be honest, I'm not keen to find myself working under Margaret after being her boss.'

Vic's voice sounded from upstairs in his bedroom.

'Dad. My train set is ready. Can I be the station master?'

'Coming,' his father called back, releasing Vera. 'We'll talk about it when the kids are in bed.'

Later, when the baby was fed and in his cot, and young Vic had had his bedtime story and was asleep, Geoff and Vera sat together on the sofa before the fire, with the dogs snoring beside them, discussing their future.

Geoff was enjoying a beer, while Vera snuggled up to him. He said, taking a sip and smacking his lips, 'I think it's just as necessary for you to continue with your career as it is with mine. We're both well qualified. The cottage is provided and it will give us the temporary home we need.'

It was quite scary for Vera to think of the completely new life ahead of them. Geoff, she detected, seemed keen to apply for the engineering job. He was well qualified and had an excellent service record, so she felt sure he would get it if he applied. But if he did, he would be far too busy with his enormous responsibility of keeping the low-lying Fenlands from flooding to help her much.

Would she be able to manage in a cottage she was sure would be run down, with two small children and so far away from her mother's house?

All the packing, ready to move, had to be done. Arrangements had to be made about shopping in an unknown rural area. And, as if that wasn't enough, she would be starting a new job, which would mean more for her to learn as well.

Geoff grabbed a tea towel and began

to dry the washed things, saying, 'You're not saying much, Vera.'

Her mind in a whirl, she answered, 'Sorry. I was just thinking what an upheaval it's going to be.'

'Things will work out,' Geoff said.

Vera gave a chuckle, she felt sure he really wanted to take the plunge. 'Oh, yes, they will — it's just a case of how they work out . . . ' She wasn't at all sure about the changes facing them. But Vera had overcome many difficulties before, and knew that for Geoff and her children she had to be just as strong to cope with this one.

Geoff rose and went over to take his pretty wife in his arms. He hugged her saying, 'Let's give it a go, eh?'

She was then quite sure he was keen to try for the engineering job — so what could she do but agree?

'I Don't Want To Let You Go'

'Congratulations!' Vera smiled proudly and kissed her husband after she learned his job interview had been successful.

Geoff smiled at his wife. He felt both pleased — and worried. He had been offered the job of overseeing some flood defences and designing the renovation and protection of the flood defences on some parts of the minor Fenland rivers. That was the part of it that was a challenge and he would find interesting.

But it was a heavy burden of responsibility he wasn't sure he should have taken on — especially as an emergency was on after the severe winter weather. Of course, taking on such an important job after his wartime experiences that had worn him down was rather a risk, too.

But he felt he could do the job helping others to prevent floods. Besides, the authorities wouldn't have given him the job if they didn't think he was capable of doing it.

Before they saw the cottage they were offered, Vera and Geoff went to the bracing seaside.

The threat of the German invasion had gone, as had the barbed wire that had covered the beaches. But standing in the strong wind that flattened their clothes to their bodies they were obliged to hold on tightly to their hats as they gazed out at the flat coastline and the steely coloured sea stretching as far as the horizon.

The vastness of the ocean was awesome. The tide was in and big waves were lively and thunderous as they fell on the beach.

Vera gasped, and joked, 'This wind will certainly get my washing dry!'

Geoff's mouth twisted into a smile. He grasped her hand and felt comforted to have Vera. She was so like her name: true and faithful — and he loved her sense of humour, which had seen them through the war years. Now she faced just as many difficulties after the war as he did.

'You don't have to live here,' he shouted above the wind, knowing he would miss her and the children terribly if she decided she couldn't face the cold bleakness.

'Are you joking?' Vera retorted, just as loudly, 'I've just got you back from the war in one piece, I don't want to let you go again.'

Geoff laughed but still felt guilty — she hadn't seen the cottage they were supposed to live in yet, but he'd been told it was in a poor condition. Seeing the power of the sea he began to be racked with doubts he dare not show Vera.

Not only was he new to this kind of engineering work, he was starting at a time after the war when much work was needed to repair the sea and river defences after the war years. Many of his workers would be German prisoners-of-war, he was told, who had no desire to help England if they could avoid it.

He pointed. 'This is where the rivers, which start up in Bedfordshire run into the sea,' he shouted as his teeth chattered. 'Water has a nasty habit of getting its own way and the Fens are as flat as pancakes.'

Vera shivered as she tried to brush a strand of hair that had blown across her face. She had to take her glove off to fix it behind her ear. 'Let's go to the hotel over there and have a bowl of soup,' she suggested, 'then we can talk in peace.'

A little later, seated in the quietness of the hotel bar, they discussed their situation.

'I wish I wasn't starting this job in wintertime,' Geoff said, taking a drink and relishing his beer. 'I should have taken up hotel management like my parents and brother.'

'That wouldn't have suited you one bit, Geoff Parkington. You'd have been bored stiff. Leave the catering side to me.'

Geoff grinned. Vera was a brilliant cook.

He appreciated Vera was being supportive — much more than many women in her position would be. Of course, his wife knew it was a job, and he needed one badly, not only for the money to pay the family bills, but to prove to himself that he could work as an engineer again.

He had met some experienced water engineers at the interview, who told him they were willing to help him learn the job, but he still felt like King Canute back there on the beach, trying to keep the tide back, especially as it was a critical time with the snow melting and water swelling the river banks which urgently needed to be made higher in places.

Indeed, no wonder they had hurriedly appointed him to lend a hand.

The food at the hotel was poor. Geoff remarked, 'I know it's difficult with food still on the ration, but I think that was one of the most awful meals I've ever had. Even the army cooks do better. There's no excuse for serving hard potatoes swimming in water and the rissoles were all gristly. I'm too used to your excellent cooking, Vera, my love.'

'I chose the fish cakes,' said Vera, 'which were a bit rubbery, overcooked, but edible.'

'I hope this meal will at least fortify us this afternoon when we go and see the cottage. I have a feeling you're not going to enjoy what you find there, either.'

Geoff felt he'd let his wife down and felt he was being honest with her.

She leant over the table and patted his hand. 'Now don't you talk like that, Geoff. We are together in this new venture and must march onwards. I am, I admit, as apprehensive as you are, but the children are young and a little hard living won't hurt them.

'They will love being by the river when the weather improves. And as for the food, why the Fens produce lovely

27

potatoes — the best in the dark soil. They just need to be cooked properly. Then there are the other fine vegetables they grow, the asparagus, which is pure luxury. Fish will be easy to get here on the coast. A bag of Norfolk shrimps are delicious.'

Trust Vera to be optimistic, he thought lovingly.

Moving On

Actually, Vera was dreading the impending move. It was not that she disliked the farming area she was moving to — it was the whole upheaval for her and her family's life after the security she'd become accustomed to.

That, and the state of the cottage which was to be her new home!

During a visit from her mother, as they sat having tea, Vera poured out her apprehension. 'Geoff has no idea how awful it is for me leaving this cosy farm cottage and going to live in that run-down place in the middle of nowhere.'

Alice Baxter tutted as she clattering her cup down on her saucer. 'I'm sure he is aware that he is placing a huge burden on you, love, but he has little option but to take that job. You know John and I'll have you and your family to live with us — you don't have to move to that place. I'm sure Geoff will manage living there by himself and visit us when he can.'

'No, thank you,' Vera said firmly. 'Geoff has been away during the war and I hated worrying about him all the time. No. I must go with him — I *want* to be with him and look after him. He needs his family around him. The boys are too small to care about the primitiveness about the place. In fact, I'm sure they will thrive in the fresh air, and playing in the river water — I'll have to keep an eye on them, though.'

She sighed. 'I'll just have to put up with the inconveniences.'

Goodness, and there were massive inconveniences! Vera dare not tell her mother about them all or she may forbid her to go there. No electricity, gas lamps had to be lit. No running water — there was a well in the garden. An outside privy and, unbelievably, an ordinary step ladder to get upstairs!

Living there — or camping more like — with Geoff was one matter. Having two young children to look after there was another kettle of fish!

But Vera was a person with massive determination, so her mother knew it was no use trying to make her change her mind.

Her mother looked sympathetically at her daughter. 'I'll miss not seeing you, dear. I always look forward to your weekly trip into Lynn with the children — and now I won't be able to see them growing up.'

It was Vera's turn to be sympathetic. 'Oh, Mum, of course you will! It's just that we won't be seeing you so often. I know it's a shame we are going to be away from a bus route, and the petrol rationing means there will be few times we can be together, but think of the summertime when we can enjoy picnics by the river.'

Vera watched her mum smile and was grateful she'd inherited her optimism and practical nature. She was glad her mother had remarried and would have her husband, John, for company.

John was a good sort and she felt sure he would save his petrol ration to bring his wife to the rural cottage whenever he could.

It was just a pity Vera had to move before the better weather began. She didn't like to mention that as she sipped her tea thoughtfully.

Her mother asked, 'Now what about this new job of yours? I expect you are delighted to be offered that.'

Vera checked her tongue. She didn't start by saying that her pride had been hurt by having to accept the job Margaret had offered her as one of her School Meals Assistants. Geoff and she needed the money so it would give them the opportunity to buy their own home.

Once again, it would mean overcoming her natural instinct to refuse and say, 'No, I don't want to live in a derelict cottage far away from the conveniences of life and you, Mum. Nor do I want to be ordered about by a bossy lady who knows far less about *catering that I do. But, I need to put up with it for my family's sake — and thank heaven Geoff has now got a job he will enjoy, so whatever work I'm asked to do I must give the impression I like it whatever it entails. I'm lucky to have such a loving family.*

Vera said, 'Well, it will take some getting used to, but at least I'll have school hours which will mean the children can be left with the baby-sitter Margaret found for me while I'm working — and Margaret does know what it is like to be a working mother.'

'You can always call on me to help out in an emergency,' said her mum.

'What emergency have you in mind?' Vera grinned thinking her coming life was going to be one of coping with one difficulty after another.

'Oh, I don't know, Vera, dear. You never know what life throws up.'

Vera avoided saying that all she had on her plate to cope with at present was more than enough and the thought of anything worse that could happen was not something she wanted to think about.

'Let's get on with the packing, Mum,' she said cheerfully getting to her feet.

★   ★   ★

Victor — Vic for short — was the apple of Vera's eye. He was going to be three in a few weeks' time and had taken after his father being bright and soldier like. His favourite gramophone record was the song, *There's something about a soldier, there's something about a soldier that is fine, fine, fine. It may be his bearing or the buttons on his coat* . . .

Vic also liked his father to play on his violin, especially the tune about *Christopher Robin's* nurse going to Buckingham Palace to see the soldiers marching about — because she was marrying one of the guards.

Young Vic had no qualms about moving to the riverside and Vera was thankful for it. He packed up his own kit bag of toys — except for his knitted penguin that Alice had made for him, because Penguin had to be hand held, and he warned the two dogs, Battle and Gyp, to be prepared for a change of billet.

On moving day, Vera looked down at small Vic, then up at Geoff as they waited for the removal van. She smiled and said, 'Well, we're ready,' and then she had to try not to break down as she felt her mouth quivering.

Geoff put his arms around her and held her tight, which didn't help as she fought not to weep. The memories of their little cottage rushed her mind. They'd been happy here. What was waiting for them now?

'The van's coming!' shouted Vic loudly and excitedly, running up to her and tugging at her skirt. Vera was thankful of the need to break away from Geoff who needed to help the men pile their packing cases into the huge van.

Vera had been so busy with the move that she'd hardly had any time to think about it recently. Baby Pete took up so much of her time, too — although, thankfully, he was an angel of a baby.

Sad goodbyes were said to neighbours the farmer and his wife, and soon they were on the road.

★ ★ ★

It was a long journey trundling behind the huge van in their car.

Vera was pleased her son was delighted with the new cottage when he saw it — so were the dogs with so many new smells to investigate.

'There's a boat,' Vic said excitedly, 'for me to play in.'

'Not until you've learnt to swim, young man!' retorted Geoff.

'I didn't know there was a river here,' said Vera.

'It's a small tributary. A backwater, but we'll have to keep an eye on the children as they are bound to want to play in it.'

Vera was cross. Not another thing for

her to worry about, she thought, but she soon forgot it because there was so much to think about. Lists had to be made, things to be organised. It just never seemed to stop.

Vera and Geoff worked with the removal men until they were exhausted, getting their things into the new cottage and trying to make it as homely as possible.

It was certainly cold. Vera shivered as she kept her coat on and didn't take Vic's off, either.

'The children will have to sleep downstairs. I can't carry the baby up and down that ladder.' Vera had to think of safety.

'And I can't get up there with Penguin in my hand,' announced Vic.

They lit the coal fire range which provided some heat in the freezing building, and then they warmed some soup Vera had prepared in the Thermos flasks.

Until it became dark they struggled to make the place habitable, and after they had put the children to bed they were soon snuggled down asleep together, too exhausted to do any more unpacking.

Back To Basics

Gone were the days when they just had to switch on the electric lights to be able to see. Vera awoke to find Geoff struggling with oil lamps.

'My goodness, what a trouble it is just to get these contraptions to work!' he exclaimed.

'Let me show you,' said Vera, reluctant to get out of bed and into the bitterly cold bedroom. 'The farmer's wife said her family used them for years before they had electricity, so she was used to using oil lighting.'

Geoff used his camp lantern to help provide some light for Vera to show him how the lamps could be lit and soon they had a glowing light in the cottage. They had some candles and candlesticks, too, of course, but naked flames could be dangerous — especially with children around.

Having let the dogs out to explore their surroundings, and hoping they would come back and they didn't have to go out and search for them, they started to get dressed.

Fortunately the children slept soundly, so Vera and Geoff were able to unpack some cooking gear and porridge was soon in a pan on the range as Geoff already had lively fires burning in the kitchen, and another in the scullery, giving warmth and hot water.

Vera smiled as she remembered the original range in the British Restaurant church hall which she had to use until it was replaced by modern ovens.

'What's amusing you?' asked Geoff as he noticed his wife's grin as she stirred the porridge.

'I was thinking how I complained about the cast-iron kitchen range at Lynn when you first showed it to me,' she replied.

Geoff chuckled as she continued, 'And it turned out to be splendid when you got used to it, as you said it was. So as this old-fashioned range here is similar, with an open fire and hot plates on top and an oven next to it. I shouldn't have much trouble cooking on it.'

'I'll buy you one of the new Calor gas cookers.'

'No, thanks — we must save our money for our new house,' replied Vera promptly. 'Anyway, if I had a new cooker I'd choose one of the new style ranges — Aga, I think they're called.'

She was determined to make the best of their new abode, which was like going back to live in the Victorian era.

She kept reminding herself that it was only temporary. She dreamt of her new house which she and Geoff would be saving hard to afford.

When Geoff had finished toasting some bread on the open fire using a toasting fork, they sat at the kitchen table and tucked into their breakfast.

Vic, with tousled hair and holding Penguin, appeared at the kitchen door in slippers and pyjamas. 'We want some breakfast,' he announced.

'Please,' corrected his father.

'Please,' repeated the little boy, 'and lots of it — we're hungry.'

Vera fed her son and listened for baby Pete to awake.

Having fortified the family with porridge and toast, Vera and Geoff began to sort out their belongings.

'I'll need to think about provisions,' Vera said, thinking out loud about her planning of food for the family and filling the store cupboard and larder.

'I'll take you into Ely to do some shopping. It's our nearest town.'

'Don't you have to go into work tomorrow?'

'Yes. The work is so urgent they only gave me two days to move.'

'It must be pressing,' remarked Vera still surrounded by a hundred and one things that she wanted to do — and wanted Geoff to do.

She knew it wouldn't be possible to keep asking him to do much more than he already had. His new job was going to take all his time and energy.

They made a list of things they wanted and put the baby in his carry cot and Vic on the back seat of the car and drove along the straight road which stood high above the lower fields each side where the peaty soil had sunk over the years.

Once in town it was a frantic time for Vera as she found a grocer's and started filling her basket with things from her list.

She had to keep an eye on Vic who wanted to help her, but kept trotting up with items she either didn't need — or couldn't afford. The grocer kindly gave Vic a barley sugar to suck — and one for Penguin — which he put in his coat pocket.

'We must get back, it's getting dark,' Geoff said as he came in the shop to settle the bill. He'd been carrying baby Pete as he went to the ironmongers to get some nails and other things he wanted for repairs for the cottage.

Vera thought it possible that she

might slap some paint on the walls which looked like they hadn't been decorated for years, but that would have to wait for the moment.

Once in the car again; it was necessary to call into the local farm and ask them to deliver some milk and eggs.

They arrived at home in darkness because they dare not drive too fast in case they all landed in a field.

Gyp and Battle were howling, unused to being left in the new place and in the dark, and needed their dinner, but the kitchen was warm and soon Vera had got busy and fed everyone — including the dogs.

'Vera,' Geoff said, when they were in bed that night, 'thanks for not making a fuss about the difficulties you're having by being here.'

Vera kissed him. 'Don't worry about me, I'll manage. The children are happy. You just concentrate on your new job now.'

'Yes. Unfortunately, I'll be up to my eyes in work from now on, but don't for one moment think that I don't appreciate your sacrifices in coming to live here. And I promise you as soon as I am able to, I'll get us out of this . . . '

'Ramshackle place?'

'Actually this cottage is well built. The Victorians made things to last. It just needs redecorating.'

'And electricity — and putting somewhere on a bus route. At present it would suit a hermit. I'm going to get bored of having to talk to myself — although Vic is quite chatty.'

Geoff chuckled and fell asleep.

Vera sighed as she stared into the darkness, always on the alert in case the baby cried downstairs, and wondered how she could possibly make a success of the School Meals Organiser job — on top of everything else.

A Challenge Awaits

As Vera waved Geoff off in the dim morning light, she hoped he would be able to manage his new position. It wasn't as if he hadn't all the engineering qualifications and experience, or that he wasn't keen to do the job — it was that he was still a little vulnerable after his war service which had drained him of his youthful vigour and injured his body and his mind. And although he was now pronounced fit by doctors, she feared he was liable to have a relapse if things got too rough . . .

It had been a difficult few months when he had returned from war duty. A haunted, distant man, Geoff had struggled to connect with the world again and the people around him.

Vera's unflinching patience and love had ensured he gradually came back to life.

Looking around at the wintery flat landscape and trees which had grown bent in the prevailing wind, Vera couldn't think of a more tedious job than looking after the rivers and their tributaries that cut though the low-lying lands.

Still, she wished she had a phone — or some way of contacting Geoff if she needed to.

'Mum, Penguin wants his breakfast!'

Vera turned to see Vic in his pyjamas — and bare feet — standing in the cold wind outside the cottage. She felt the urge to scold him for being out in the cold, but in a way she was pleased he was a tough little lad — dirty clothes and feet didn't prevent Vic from playing boisterous games and enjoying himself.

Hustling him indoors, she soon organised breakfast for the children.

Having made the beds and had a general tidy up, she went back into the kitchen to make a cup of tea.

She jumped as she heard someone enter the cottage and became aware of feet pounding towards her.

Swinging around she saw it was Margaret and she removed her hand from over her mouth as she said, 'Gracious me! You gave me a fright, Margaret! Why didn't you ring the bell or knock or something?'

'Don't be so touchy! There wasn't a bell I could see,' retorted her tall friend. 'Besides, as far as I can see there isn't anything here that a burglar would want to pinch anyway!'

'Oh, thanks!' Vera said with a broad smile, knowing inside she was pleased to see her friend, who could be rather forthright.

'My goodness, you do live in the back of beyond!' exclaimed Margaret as she flopped down in a chair without being asked.

Vera laughed. 'You found us anyway. What about a cup of tea?'

'And a biscuit — if you've got such a thing in this god-forsaken place.'

There she was, ordering her about again, but Vera wasn't sorry to sit down for a chat.

Margaret confessed to her, 'I'm feeling a bit fragile this morning . . . '

Vera grinned as she made the tea, 'Why's that?'

'I've just left Deanna at school — her first day.'

Vera nodded sympathetically. 'I'm sure I'll be feeling the same about Vic when he goes off to school — although he's a soldier's boy.'

As Vera put the kettle on Margaret said, 'I passed Geoff driving along the High Street in Ely. I waved to him, but he didn't notice me — he looked pretty intense and preoccupied.'

'It's his first day at work, too.'

'Ah, and next week it'll be yours!'

Vera almost dropped the tea pot.

'Yes, I managed to get a lady to fill your post until next week when you'll be taking over. I've come to tell you about it.'

'Wow! Hold on.' Vera's hand rattled the cup as she handed the cup and saucer to Margaret. 'I haven't agreed to take the job yet.'

Margaret took a sip of tea. 'Well,' she said, looking around at the packing cases, 'It won't take you long to empty these cases. And when you've done that — what are you going to do with yourself all day?'

'Look after my children, for a start.'

'I've found you a baby-sitter. A really nice woman. Mrs Enid Perrot. Loves children. You'll like her. She's been looking after Deanna for me. In fact, when we've had tea we'll take the children over to Ely to meet her — she's expecting you — and you can decide.'

Me, decide? Thought Vera with raised eyebrows. It sounded as if everything was already decided. But did she really mind? She agreed with Margaret that she wouldn't find a lot to occupy herself when the unpacking was finished. Besides, the sooner she made some money and got out of this cottage into a new house the better, and if Margaret had arranged everything — well, it meant that she wouldn't have to, would she?

'And . . . ' Margaret said, munching

into a biscuit, 'you'll get a car from the council car pool.'

'Wow!' Vera took a gulp of tea. 'Really? That's wonderful!'

Having a car, and petrol to run it, was a real incentive. She could visit her mother on occasions. 'Margaret,' she said, suddenly serious, 'you'd better tell me about the job.'

'It'll be a breeze for you, Vera. Inspecting school kitchens, keeping the cooks up to scratch, making sure the school meals are nutritious, and following government guidelines. You'll suggest improvements and all that sort of thing. It's perfect for you. You know your stuff, girl.'

Vera had to agree having a Cordon Bleu cooking qualification was more than she needed to do a job like that, and after years of running a British Restaurant as well, it would make the job seem relatively easy for her.

Margaret added, 'And, the hours are less than a full-time job would be, because you can do some of your office work at home. It really is a great opportunity. It'll keep you ticking over.'

It seemed as though Margaret had thought of everything — including the dogs who, being older, would be all right left at home during her short working hours.

'OK, I'll seriously consider it,' Vera said resignedly. 'Geoff isn't against me working,' she added. Although she knew Geoff would be more pleased if she were able to take a job that advanced her career.

★　★　★

With the children well wrapped up, they all got into Margaret's car and set off to see Enid Perrot. With an impressive cathedral in the centre of Ely, the area around it had many old houses, which made the city seem full of character.

Mrs Perrot was plump, jolly, and used to minding children. She and Vic hit it off at once because Penguin was accepted as the little boy's friend, and baby Pete seemed content to be in Enid's arms.

Not that Vera wanted to leave her children for part of each day — or even her dogs — but having weighed up the advantages she would have by taking the job, Vera could only thank Margaret for arranging everything to make it possible for her.

However, as Margaret then explained the School Meals Organiser's job, Vera felt overwhelmed by all she needed to learn.

Vera thumbed through the huge file of official papers she had to read about the job, with charts showing how much protein, fat, etc each child should have per meal, and the map showing which school kitchens she had to visit each week.

She felt like a winded fighter.

$\star \quad \star \quad \star$

Later that day, Geoff arrived home equally as tired and dejected. It was all Vera could do to sound positive about her job, when all that occupied Geoff was the precariousness of the river banks — and the need to build them up quickly before the snows melted and the rivers became swollen with extra water and flooding occurred over the flat Fenlands.

Vera could sense she must push aside her own worries and not put any more pressure on Geoff, but she did worry about their relationship. Once before in her life — when Geoff had been injured during the war, she had lost him. And now she feared with the enormous responsibilities they both faced it was easy to slip back into bad habits.

Perhaps she shouldn't have taken the job Margaret had offered her? She should be there for Geoff and not making more demands on her own time.

And yet Vera could see the positive side of being away from the cottage for a few hours each day.

She concentrated on them as she explained to Geoff, 'I'll be meeting people and making sure the schoolchildren are given nutritious meals, just as I did before as a British Restaurant cook.'

His endearing worried-looking expression stayed throughout their conversation, although he nodded.

'The children took to Mrs Perrot, their baby-sitter. I feel confident because Margaret allowed her to look after little Deanna, so she will be fine with Vic and Pete, too.'

Geoff listened to Vera's description of Mrs Perrot and her home and agreed his children would be happy there. It was all a bit new to him, though. Things were changing faster than he could keep up. The world was a different place and people had changed over the war years. Nothing would ever be the same again. Paid baby-sitters indeed!

Vera's eyes sparkled. 'And I'll be given a car — a little Morris Minor, which are very reliable — and petrol.'

Geoff smiled wanly.

'We'll be able to save some money towards our new house!'

'That will be useful.'

The fact that he didn't sound too enthusiastic, Vera put down to the fact that he had his own new job to mull over.

Geoff described his first day at work as tiring, and Vera could see the strain showing. 'There is so much for me to learn, and the rivers are brimming full, which makes the situation dangerous . . .' his voice trailed off as he sat staring into space, pondering the problem.

'Can you do it?'

'Oh, yes.'

'Have you the workers to do it?'

Geoff looked at her as he nodded. 'Local Fenmen are helping with the sacks of gault, so that's something.'

'What's that?'

'Gault is a local word used for earth — a mix of clay and soil — very heavy stuff.'

'You can't haul that around!'

'I don't have to. The army has sent troops — and prisoners of war and I'm impressed as they are working hard. The problem I have is deciding where the banks need reinforcing.'

Vera looked at him sympathetically. She didn't like to ask if they were in an area likely to flood, but she was sure Geoff would know that. It was bad enough that there was a severe winter this year, with the rivers already so high. Quite a way to start his job.

Fortunately, Geoff mentioned one young engineer, Dickie Brightman, who seemed keen to help him learn about the job, so that was a great help in these early days where he was learning so much as he went along.

In the late evening, a light shone over the huge maps he was studying as he planned how he was going to strengthen the river banks in the places he'd been assigned to.

It was far too important work for Vera to interrupt him — so she told him that there would be enough water for him to have a bath if he only ran the hot tap, and went to have a wash before she climbed into their cold bed hugging a hot-water bottle.

An Evacuation

With a few days to go before she started work, Vera concentrated on planning her new life as a working mum.

Delighted to have a Morris Minor pool car available for her use, it soon became part of her life and she called it Mickey Mouse, after Walt Disney's cartoon character. Having a car made things easier for shopping without bothering Geoff, whose exhausting work was taking up all of his time.

The children settled down well with their new babysitter and apart from the time it took her to take them over to Ely and back home again, Vera spent some time in the School Meals Service Office and began to read all the information she'd been given by the Ministry of Food on providing meals for school-children — and visiting the schools in the district to meet the canteen staff.

Margaret rang the office with more instructions about the latest food-rationing points and sent her charts for her to put up on her kitchen walls showing how much of the basic foods were to be in each child's meal.

'Don't send me any more,' Vera begged. 'We haven't the wall space in the kitchens.'

'They are *official*, Vera. From the Ministry and they send round inspectors every so often.'

'Wow!' breathed Vera, 'Do they have panting dogs with big teeth to make sure you've papered your walls properly?'

Margaret was not amused

'Now look here, Vera. You're no longer in charge. I am. What I say goes.'

'OK. OK. I'll stick 'em up — somewhere.'

Margaret huffed. 'I have enough trouble trying to work out the budget and where to obtain the food the kitchens need. I was going to ask you about where to obtain some sausages . . . '

Vera could believe Margaret had an important job — but she resented being put down by her friend. After the war, restrictions and rules were bad enough without making them seem worse, and being heavy handed with those who work with you was not necessary — even if you are the boss. Unless, of course, some employee does something really wrong that has to be sorted out.

But Vera saw no point in resenting Margaret's position and quarrelling with her. Margaret had helped her get a job after all. Even if she was being asked to do part of Margaret's job as well.

'Sausages? Yes, well, I realise the funding makes it difficult in rural areas to find suppliers for small schools, but I'll ask around this area and let you know.'

★　★　★

It was a challenge, but after a few days working Vera found it interesting, as her willingness to help the cooks with the problems they had soon made her welcome wherever she went.

'I'm just a dogsbody,' Vera explained to her mother on the phone from the office. 'I get called on if a member of the staff is away to go help peel spuds. Then I have to cart a crate of cabbages from one canteen to another if one has too many and another not enough. I get emergency calls because the sausages have been burnt to a cinder — and they don't know how to cope with the crisis. And now the Ministry intends to begin installing new kitchen equipment and I have to explain to the staff how to use it.'

Alice sounded a little sad. 'It sounds as if you don't have time to come and see me at present. And the weather has been so awful.'

Vera sighed. She could imagine her mum was housebound and bored. 'You and John can always pop over and see us.'

'Not at the minute. The weather

61

forecast is dire. We'd land up in a ditch at the side of those long, straight Fen roads.'

Vera agreed that her elderly mother and step-father might swerve off the slippery icy roads in their little car, and so she didn't encourage them to make the journey.

Nor did she mention how worried she was becoming about the thaw setting in and the extremely high river and ditch water levels — that concerned Geoff, too.

'I think you should go and stay with your mother,' Geoff said one evening. 'In fact, I insist you do. I'm afraid of this storm that's coming. The radio mentioned it on the news.'

Vera listened to the fierce wind howling outside and didn't like the sound of it one bit. 'I suppose it is March roaring in like a lion.'

Geoff finished his meal, not saying he'd enjoyed it as he usually did. 'That's right. But you know there is an emergency on at present. The flow of water coming down from upcountry because of the thaw, and going into the already swollen rivers is putting the flood banks under strain. And now this storm . . . yes, I think you must take the children over to Alice in the morning and stay there with them until things quieten down.'

Vera didn't argue. Although she had no phone to ring her mum from the cottage, she knew her mother would be pleased to see her and the children and have them for a few days until the water subsided.

'OK. I'll get a few things packed,' she said. 'What about you?'

'Dickie Brightman, that bright spark from my office, has offered to put me up in Ely for a while.'

'That's nice of him.'

'Yes, it will make things easier for me at work, too, if I'm on the spot.' Geoff looked affectionately at his wife. 'Although,' he said, 'I hate to be parted from you and the children, love.'

Vera, too, hated the thought of being

parted from him. She could tell, looking at the strain on his face, he was under terrific nervous tension and really needed her.

But what else could she do but agree to pack up and go and stay with her mum — for a while at least?

So, having made the decision to part in the morning, they planned to leave the cottage during the bad weather.

★   ★   ★

The night's storm hadn't gone away. It had actually become worse.

The high sea tides rushed into the wash and everywhere water could go became saturated. Rivers and their tributaries filled up with surging water as the wind howled across the flat Fenlands.

Geoff looked out of the cottage window as soon as it became light. 'I don't like the look of this weather,' he said. 'We must get going as soon as we can.'

Vera found getting the children, and herself, ready to leave took time, especially as she sensed Geoff was anxious for her to be faster.

He wanted to be off.

'I'll take baby Pete over to your mother's,' Geoff announced, swallowing a hurried breakfast cup of tea. 'You'll have enough to do coping with Vic and the dogs in your car.'

Geoff had to leave straight away. He had a long drive to Lynn before he could double back to his job in Ely where he was needed.

Outside in the biting wind and slanting sheets of rain, they bundled the baby in his carry-cot, and then into Geoff's car.

'I don't like to leave you here alone,' Geoff shouted above the wind. 'Follow me as soon as you can.'

'Oh, I will.'

He turned to face her and placed his hands firmly on her shoulders. 'Promise me you'll get going as soon as you can, in fact, within the next few minutes. I don't want you here any longer than necessary.'

'I promise.'

He kissed her quickly, saying, 'If I don't see you for a while, you know I'll be thinking of you and the children, and I'm relieved you'll be with your mother.'

As he got into his car she called, 'And you take care, my love.'

He gave a wave. They didn't need to say much, their love was understood between them, and as Vera stood in the gusty wind and rain and watched his car get smaller and smaller as it disappeared along the long straight road into the distance, she felt a sudden dread.

Seeing them going away made her realise how precious her husband and baby son were to her.

Because of Geoff's strong warning she knew she had to get away from the cottage as soon as possible. Was it because he feared the area was liable to flood at this time with the extraordinary high water level?

She gave a shudder — yes, it could be.

So get on she must, and make a start on her journey. She had her other young son to think of.

Move yourself, Vera, right now!

'Vic!' she shouted, running into the cottage, 'Get up. We're going off early this morning.'

Then she stopped and caught her breath. With her hand on her beating heart she tried to calm down. Geoff hadn't been in the slightest panicky — so neither must she.

Upsetting her little boy would be silly. He wasn't a nervous child, but it would be better to hide her fears from him.

So, fighting her secret fear with trying to think what had to be done, Vera spent the next few minutes getting her son dressed and explaining the situation.

'We're going to see Granny this morning — and we're staying in Lynn for a while.'

'Goody!' Vic gave her a wide smile. 'I haven't seen Granny for ages.'

Vera swept his hair from his forehead and gave him a kiss. 'I'll put out some milk and cornflakes for you while I get a few things in the car. We must leave at once.'

Collecting what she considered essential to take with them, Vera looked quickly around the cottage in a panic.

Everything in her home was important to her — simple things for the most part, but things she didn't want to leave behind, but knew she had to. As Vic finished his breakfast she said, 'Get your favourite toys to take to Granny's, will you? Put them in this bag.'

Vic did as he was told, trotting about to collect his toys and books, while Vera managed to take a few things she could manage up the ladder where she thought that they might not get soaked if the cottage did get flooded downstairs.

Vic, well wrapped up in his raincoat, hat and with wellies, and clutching his woolly penguin, was put in the back seat of the car. But as Vera was about to shut him in, he started to yell, 'Let me get out! Let me out! I must get Dad's violin. He needs it.'

Oh dear! Vic was right. Geoff did enjoy playing his violin. Music had been a great help in his recovery after the war. She remembered where he kept it downstairs on the ground floor.

'I'll get it,' she shouted and dived back into the cottage, grabbed the violin case and hugged it to herself as she struggled to make her way back to the car while the wind kept tugging at her hand, trying to blow it away before she managed to push it into the boot.

It wasn't until she was seated in the driver's seat of the car again that she remembered the dogs.

They had gone off for their usual early morning exploration — and hadn't returned.

With everything packed into the car, and Vic with his penguin peering out of the car window she wanted to be off.

She needed to leave. The wind was persistent and the rain beating down. Mercilessly.

But where were the two dogs?

Vera got out of the car and struggled in the powerful wind around the cottage calling them frantically.

'Gyp! Battle! Where are you? Gyp, come back here now!'

But the loud sounds of the gusty wind seemed to drown her shouts.

Her heart was beating fast. How Vera loved her dogs — so did Geoff and Vic. She couldn't leave them behind.

And yet . . . how long could she wait for them? She had already delayed much longer that she'd promised Geoff she would.

She knew she must think of her family — Geoff and the children came first. She was sure Geoff was well on the way to her mother's house with baby Pete by now.

She had little Victor in the car and it was her responsibility to get him away from this stormy area and safely

delivered to her mum's. She'd promised
Geoff she would not hang about . . . but
how hard it was to decide to leave without her pets.

What a dreadful dilemma. The poor
animals would come home and find the
family gone! And dogs couldn't climb
the cottage ladder to get away from
flood water.

Waiting for the dogs to appear was
sheer agony. She felt herself beginning
to panic and took some deep breaths.

'For goodness' sake, come back here
now!' she shouted into the wind, which
only howled back at her.

But they didn't return and Vera knew
she had to leave them behind.

Sobbing, Vera got into the car's driving seat and started the engine. Between
huge gulps she drove slowly away from
the cottage with the windscreen wipers
flashing to and fro in front of her.

Every now and then a blast of wind
caught the car and rocked it.

'Mum! Mum!' she heard Vic's urgent
voice from the back seat. 'Stop!'

Turning around she saw her little boy pointing as he looked out of the back window. 'Gyp's running after the car.'

Stopping with a screech of breaks, Vera got out of the car to see Gyp come panting up, and way far behind him like a speck in the distance came Battle, Geoff's old Labrador, lumbering as fast as he could.

It was just as well it was raining as the wetness on her face hid her tears. She didn't want Vic to notice how upset she was.

Gyp had belonged to her first boyfriend, Bill, who was killed during the war. She'd promised Bill to look after his dog before he went to Malta.

The dog arrived at the car soaking wet and tail wagging. Vera opened the door to let him in and Vic squealed as the soaking wet dog greeted him with licks.

She really shouldn't wait about. The rain was becoming so heavy she could hardly see and she knew she should have been away long before this. But dear old Battle was obviously struggling to get to them as fast as he could.

Every minute was painful for Vera having to wait when her instinct told her they should be off.

At last the exhausted animal finally reached the car.

Getting the heavy wet animal up into the small car wasn't easy, but as the drenched dog was just as anxious to squeeze himself in it helped with the effort.

'The dogs are all dirty and wet, Mum. Their claws are scratching my legs.'

Vera sympathised. The short trousers boys wore offered no protection for poor Vic's legs as they trampled all over him.

'Yes, I'm sorry Vic. I haven't a dog towel to dry them. But be a brave soldier and put up with it. I'll get you cleaned up when we reach Granny's house.'

'That'll be ages. I'm sh-shivering.'

'Soldiers do get cold at times, Vic.'

'Penguin doesn't like it.'

'Yes, he does. Penguins love the water.'

They were off at last. Much later than she'd hoped.

As they drove along, strong gusts of wind buffeted the small car alarmingly. What bothered Vera more was that she found it difficult to see out of the wind-screen because the rain and the water on the road was making it impossible for her to see where she was going.

Vera clenched the driving wheel. If she wasn't careful she could drive the car off the road, which was higher than the fields on either side of it. They could all land up in the deep water-filled ditch at the side of the road!

All she knew for sure was that the road was straight. All she must do is to drive along it, straight ahead.

Vera felt her eyes sore from straining to see ahead as the windscreen wipers couldn't move faster enough to clear the screen properly.

A Dangerous Journey

'There's something about a soldier, there's something about a soldier, that is fine, fine, fine.' Vic's piping voice in the little car was a comfort to Vera as she drove forward in the blinding rain.

She went along this road every day. The trees that lined the road showed where it was, but the uncertainty of knowing where the edge was made her feel shaky.

So much water was about it seemed as if they were in a boat as they waded through it. Biting her lip Vera kept her foot gently down on the accelerator and crawled along at about ten miles an hour.

Soon they were almost at a crossroads and as she approached it she began to ask herself if she should continue going across the Fenlands towards Lynn. It wasn't at all pleasant driving in the pouring rain. Perhaps they would be better turning towards Ely and going to Enid Perrot's.

Ely was built on one of the few hills in the Fenlands. The old name, Ely, meant island and all Vera could think of was getting up out of the low-lying area.

'I think as it's raining so much we'd better go to Mrs Perrot's.'

'OK, Mum. Penguin likes Mrs Perrot. But we want to go and see Granny later.'

'Yes, dear, we will.'

Vera was worried that Enid Perrot may not appreciate having two wet dogs in her house, but she reasoned that she could take them to her office — and hope Margaret didn't make a fuss about them.

She was pleased she'd made the decision to go to Ely when she saw the cathedral, known as the 'Ship of the Fens', standing up in the distance. It was like a goal to reach. Pilgrims had been coming to Ely for years to find solace in the magnificent cathedral and Vera took comfort from its strength and presence.

They still had to reach the city, however, and the water on the car tyres and on the road made it feel like they were driving through a river.

She wondered if she should drive towards the nearest house and ask the occupants to give them shelter, but she was so near her destination now. She must drive on then phone her mum as she would be expecting them and would be waiting anxiously. She should also phone Geoff's office, to let him know what had happened to her.

Geoff would be so worried — and he could do without that emotional pressure at this crucial time when it was becoming clear to Vera that the river at Ely was flooding . . .

★　★　★

Indeed Geoff feared the water was at the top of the river flood banks, and as the land behind the banks was so much lower, it didn't take long for water to begin spilling over the flat land.

Even before Geoff had reached Lynn with his baby in his car, he was caught in a dilemma because he knew the situation was quickly becoming very dangerous and he should really be in his office in Ely taking charge of the situation in his area.

He blamed himself for not warning Vera earlier. He knew how serious the flooding could be and now he could see how his worst fears were coming true. The River Ouse was overflowing into the flat countryside. Some of the banks had been unable to contain all the extra water rushing down from Bedfordshire, and together with the high tides it had made the flooding start.

Gripping the steering wheel, he told himself to concentrate on one thing at a time.

Aware he was vulnerable to stress, he had to calm himself. Nothing would be achieved if he lost control.

He must not think he was responsible for nature's fury. He was new to the job and had done his best to protect his river banks. Even the workers had to give up in places because they couldn't stand up in the fierce winds as they strove to make the banks higher with sandbags.

If he had done anything wrong it was not moving his family to Lynn earlier — and not being in the office right now to cope with the critical situation.

But right now he had his baby son in the back of his car, and the child must be taken to safety.

Get to Lynn first.

After a while baby Pete seemed to sense the tension, and began to whimper and then bawl, but Geoff drove on, determinedly.

Although it seemed to take for ever, he was soon outside his in-laws' house.

A Helping Hand

John answered the urgent ringing of the front door bell in his dressing gown and pyjamas and looked amazed to see Geoff's wet and strained face — with the crying baby in his arms.

Geoff shouted above the child's shrill racket, 'Look after Pete, will you? The river's flooding — we had to leave the cottage. The whole place is becoming dangerous. I need to get back.'

John, being an ex-soldier, saw the wet and distraught expression on Geoff's face and accepted the child, and his carry cot, which was pushed into his hands.

Vera's mother, Alice, with curlers in her hair, came downstairs to see what all the commotion was about. She called out, 'Where's little Victor — and Vera?'

'On their way, Alice, don't worry. I came ahead. Sorry I can't stop — I must get back to Ely immediately.' Geoff gasped for breath, 'The situation is critical.'

He didn't wait around. Running back to his car he was soon heading back towards Ely, splashing along the roads as fast as he dare.

Passing horse-drawn farm carts that contained people with their belongings and searching for higher land, he hoped at any minute to see Vera's car approaching Lynn.

Vera, meanwhile, was struggling to drive her car through the increasingly flooding roads — and just about managing to keep her racing emotions in check.

She wasn't doing as she'd been told and gone off to Lynn a few minutes after Geoff left, as she'd promised she would. She'd have been there by now if she had.

She hadn't gone towards Lynn at all.

Ely lay ahead — the cathedral on the horizon appeared larger as she approached the city — and under normal conditions it would be her usual run to her baby-sitter's house and her office. But today was different.

It was extraordinarily wet and windy.

Even worse, she had to accept that as her little car was approaching the town's River Ouse, they were driving — or wading through deep water. It was taking ages to move forward. She looked at her watch. It was mid morning already.

Vic piped up, 'Mum, Mum, are we in the river? There are some ducks on the road.'

Sure enough Vera could see a couple of ducks bobbing about on the water in front of the car.

The dogs had noticed the ducks, too, and began to bark excitedly.

She was tempted to shout at the lot of them to shut up, but it was important for her not to show her little son she was in a panic.

'We are almost at Mrs Perrot's house now,' she croaked. The place seemed still too far away.

It was when the car refused to go any further that she closed her eyes and prayed.

'God, what shall I do?'

The water wasn't so deep that she couldn't get out and walk. Perhaps they ought to?

But as Vera looked around she wondered where could they go?

The owners of nearby houses wouldn't appreciate her carload dumped on them. They would be busy trying to get their own possessions upstairs out of the way of the rising water.

Pressing onwards in the car had now become unwise. Vera could get out and walk through the water and so could Vic and the dogs . . . but soon the grim reality of a long walk wading through the water to the riverside house became clear.

How could she carry all the bags that were in the car?

Her heart thumped as she stopped the car and held her hand on her heaving chest. She was fighting to keep composed as Vic wanted to know why they had parked before they got to Mrs Perrot's house.

Vera sat in a daze wondering what to do.

Suddenly she was aware of something looming up by the side of her car.

A huge shire farm horse turned to look down at her and tossed its head.

Vic shrieked in delight. The dogs barked incessantly. Someone opened her car door. 'Get yourself out and into my wagon,' ordered a wrinkled-faced old man.

'But I have a child and dogs.'

'I can sees that, missus. There's plenty of room for 'em all.'

In the next few minutes Vera was too stunned to do more than park the car at the side of the road and with the farmer's help get them up into the farm wagon, which contained some of his possessions, as well as a few muddy sugar beet. It was sturdy transport — but far from clean.

'Can I get up with the driver?' asked Vic.

'No,' Vera said sharply, and wished she hadn't sounded so cross. She was still in shock, and knew her little boy had been good, cheerfully helping to empty the car of their things, and was now clutching his father's violin case as well as his toy penguin.

His wide smile seemed to show he was enjoying the last part of the journey in a horse and cart, and made Vera feel proud of him.

The dogs sniffed around and settled down after the cart was pulled forward with a jerk and Vera lost her balance.

'Whoops-a-daisy!' Vera had fallen over, making her mac as filthy as the wagon. She decided to stay sitting down looking backwards of the cart, and as the horse plodded forward she watched her little car becoming smaller in the distance — wondering sadly if she'd lost her little Mickey Mouse for ever.

There was no doubt that the water on the road by the river was rising. Vera knew she had done the right thing to abandon her car.

There was a sudden shriek.

Alarmed, Vera's head twisted around to see Vic leaning over the side of the wagon, red faced in rage. 'Stop! Stop! I want to get out!'

'What's the matter?'

The boy had difficulty speaking as he pointed outside the cart.

Vera got to her feet and looking over the side of the cart and saw Penguin floating on the water.

'Penguin fell out of my hand when I was leaning over the cart.' Vic sobbed.

'He's swimming well,' said Vera, partly out of helplessness. How could she retrieve his woolly toy? It was just fortunate Geoff's violin hadn't fallen in the water.

'I want my Penguin.' Vic's anguished voice made the driver turn to see what was the matter.

Vera called to the driver, 'Please stop. My son's knitted toy has fallen off the wagon,'

There was a sudden loud splash, and Vera watched in alarm as she saw Battle the Labrador had jumped off the side of the cart and was wading through the water to grab Penguin in his mouth then he turned to swim back to the wagon.

'Hurrah, Hurrah!' shouted Vic, turning his crying into a grin of joy.

But getting near the wagon as it moved forward was making it difficult for poor old Battle. So Vera yelled again for the driver to stop.

The driver halted the horse and getting down from the perch he waded around to see the reason for the commotion.

'I wish he'd caught a pheasant!' the farmer grumbled. Then, wading over to the dog, he grasped Battle firmly around his middle and lifted the soaking dog up on to the wagon. 'Now you cling hold of that dog of yours, young man. I can't keep stopping — this ain't a ruddy bus.'

Battle dropped Penguin in front of the delighted boy and wagged his tail, then proceeded to shake himself, spraying Vera and her belongings.

In reply to her protests, the farmer grinned and said, 'A bit of water won't hurt you, Missus. Now where do you want to be dropped off?'

Vera thought quickly. There was no point in going on to Enid Perrot's house now. Enid would be in turmoil living so near the river, and wouldn't expect or want them to arrive. It was a good way to her office from where they now stood and she was wet and filthy and so was Vic.

Suddenly she remembered there was a primary school she visited nearby. It was up on a hill and would be away from the floods.

'I'd like to get to that school up there,' she said, pointing to the building. 'If it's not too out of your way.'

'That'll be extra,' the farmer said, winking at Vic who was clutching his wet toy penguin and telling him off for falling in the water.

However, the farmer did kindly set his horse to toil up the incline, and when they arrived there he deposited

Vera, her son, dogs and luggage outside the school entrance before he clambered up to his driving seat, and after refusing a fare for the ride, he turned the horse around and began plodding down the hill.

Vera took a quick look around to make sure she had everything and regretted how bedraggled she looked. She'd never turned up for work before looking so dirty. She breathed a sigh of relief. 'Well, at least we're all safe and sound,' she muttered.

Vic looked at her with a puzzled expression on his young face. 'What do you mean, Mum? We've had a wonderful morning — an adventure! I going to tell Dad all about it.'

Vera put her arm around him. 'Let's go in and dry out.'

'Yes, Penguin's quite wet.'

'Yes, I would agree, he's dripping, but then we all are.'

Vic's beaming smile as he looked up at his mother gave Vera a sense of the reality. They were in a dreadful state, but it was a most unusual situation. They were all safe and sound which was the main thing, and the high ground they were now on should keep them safe.

What the head teacher would say when she saw them all she dreaded to think!

Sanctuary

The caretaker had opened the Roundwood School gates and heated the building well before nine o'clock, ready for a normal school day — although it was not. Very few children turned up, only those who lived near the school and the same applied to the staff.

The head teacher, Miss Smith, knew Vera, and although she looked disapprovingly at all the baggage Vera had brought with her that morning — and particularly at the wet dogs who had no leads and were sniffing around — she didn't refuse her sanctuary.

'I'm ever so sorry,' Vera said with an apologetic smile. 'We had to abandon our cottage this morning and as you can see I wasn't able to reach my mum's house to find shelter.'

'We had an adventure,' piped up Vic. Miss Smith loved children and immediately took to the bright little boy as he described what had happened to them that morning, even showing her his father's violin, which he proudly said he'd saved.

'Well, Victor, you've done your good deed for the day. Now, how would you like to join the other children in the hall? They're playing games in there this morning.'

Vic looked up at his mother and when Vera nodded he beamed, saying, 'Yipee!'

Vera whispered to Miss Smith, 'I ought to dry him out first. His comfort toy is soaked.'

'He's had a swim,' said Vic, holding up his sodden toy, Penguin.

Miss Smith agreed. 'We'll put him on the radiator to dry off, shall we?'

'It might be too hot for him.'

'I'll keep an eye on him. Now take off your rain things and let me take you to the hall and introduce you to our teachers and children.'

She said to Vera aside, 'He'll soon dry

out running about.'

Vera was so thankful to see Vic being marched off happily towards the hall with Miss Smith.

In a minute or two when Miss Smith came back, Vera asked if she could go to the kitchen and help prepare a midday meal for all the children and staff who'd turned up.

'That would be most kind of you, Mrs Parkington. I doubt if our cook will be able to get here if the river is flooding and the children in the hall will be hungry after all the exercise they're getting this morning. After lunch I'll have to see about getting them all home early today.'

Only too pleased to think she could be useful in return for the hospitality she was being offered, Vera first asked if she could use the school phone, which was in the headmistress's study.

Miss Smith said yes, and that she would go off and find the caretaker and ask him if he would help Vera.

When she rang Geoff's office she got no reply.

Then ringing her mother, she was pleased to know Geoff had delivered the baby, who she was told was now gurgling happily on his grandmother's knee after having been fed.

'Geoff left immediately after dropping off the baby,' Alice said. 'He looked dreadfully worried.'

'He would be,' said Vera, 'there's an emergency on — extensive flooding.'

'Oh, dear me. Yes, John heard about it on the wireless. Are you all right?'

'Yes, Mum. I'm in Ely.' She went on quickly to tell her that she still planned to make her way to Mrs Perrot's house so she could tell Geoff in case he rang her wanting to find out where she'd got to.

Vera didn't want to worry her mother about how bad the situation was becoming around Ely.

She hoped the river at Lynn would not flood and felt thankful to know her baby would be well looked after by her mother and step-father.

However, she was worried about Geoff. Would he be able to stand up to the stress of seeing the powerful pressure of the water pressing against the river banks — and not give way himself?

Geoff was vulnerable, she knew, but surely he would realise the flooding was an act of God? The rush of water coming down from Bedfordshire, the yearly high tides, and the terrific storm last night had all come together. It was a disaster — no-one's fault. Geoff, new to the job, had done his best in the short time he'd had to reinforce the banks.

'Oh, my dearest Geoff. Please don't blame yourself, my darling,' she muttered. 'Look after yourself.' She closed her eyes.

'Are you all right, Mrs Parkington?' asked the headmistress, who had returned to her room.

'Yes, thank you. I was just saying a prayer out loud for my husband.'

'Where is he?'

'Out in the floods — somewhere.'

They looked at each other with grave faces.

'Well, I can't help him at the moment,' Vera said, 'so I'd better start cooking.'

At that moment the caretaker came along and offered to carry some of Vera's things into the kitchen. Vera called the dogs and when they went into the kitchen, Vera sighed with relief. Kitchens were her domain.

'Where shall I put the dogs?'

'In the boiler room, Mrs Parkington. I'll find some old cloths for them to snuggle down on. They'll be warm and cosy — and safe in there.'

'That's kind of you, thanks,' Vera said, 'Poor old Battle is asleep on his paws.'

Well, Vera decided, instead of making myself sick with worry about Geoff, I'll worry instead about getting a meal ready for about fifty or sixty children, and a few adults. But first I'll make a cup of tea, and while the kettle's boiling, I'll check the food store and see what I can find for everyone to eat. All the school kitchens had emergency stores.

The caretaker had unlocked the kitchen and given Vera the spare storeroom keys. Vera got on with making tea for herself, the caretaker and the teachers, while the caretaker took the crates containing the third-of-a-pint bottles of free school milk into the hall for the children.

Refreshed after her cuppa, Vera smiled as she saw the assistant cook come into the kitchen and look alarmed to see her there.

'Mrs Parkington, it's nice to see you, but I'm surprised you've come in this weather,' she said, looking up at the kitchen clock. 'I'm sorry to be so late.'

Vera smiled at the young woman. 'Don't be. You did well to come. Josey Willow, aren't you?'

After Josey agreed she was, Vera said, 'I'm only here because I couldn't drive though the flood to my baby-sitter.' Her face fell. Enid Perrot — she hadn't let her know where she was in case Geoff rang her to check she was all right because she'd told her mother she was still going to the baby-sitter!

'Oh, blimey! I've forgotten to ring her. I'd better do it right away.'

Josey said, 'What shall I start doing? Cook hasn't come and I don't think she'll be able to get here anyway.'

'I understand it would be difficult for her, so you and I will have to knock a meal up for everyone.'

The dinner lady looked startled, asking, 'Can you cook, Mrs Parkington?'

Vera chuckled. 'Just about. Now, there's a cup of tea if you'd like one, then get some spuds peeled, please — and some carrots.'

* * *

As Vera knocked on the head's door she wished she hadn't gone to disturb her.

Fortunately the headmistress allowed Vera to use her phone, provided she made it a quick call, because she wanted to use it to contact some parents about the children being sent home from school early.

'Enid, are you all right?'

Vera heard her huff. 'Not really, our garden is flooding and the water is coming in downstairs . . . I've got the kids upstairs, but wish I had someone here to help me lift the furniture off the floor. I'm trying to save what I can.'

Vera said she wouldn't keep her and wished she was there to help.

'Oh, Mrs Parkington. Your husband rang to ask if you were with me. He sounded worried. He said you were supposed to be with your mother but hadn't turned up. Your mother had told him that you might be on your way here, but I told him that you weren't with me. I had to say I hadn't a clue where you were.'

'If he rings again, say I'm at Roundwood School, will you?'

Vera felt like crying. She'd missed the opportunity to reassure Geoff that she, Vic, and the dogs were safe, although she'd had to abandon the car. It was all she could do to thank the headmistress again and slide out of the study door trying her best to compose herself as she made her way back to the kitchen.

To start with, what could she find for them to eat? Back in the kitchen she tried to dismiss every other worry from her mind as she washed her hands and put on an overall, then went to look in the kitchen store.

After a short look around another disaster hit Vera. There wasn't much in there. The stores were very low. Why on earth was there so little of almost everything?

Basic ingredients were allowed for schools and this enabled the cooks to make good quality, nutritious meals for the children each day. She had charts issued to her showing what each child should get.

But how could this kitchen store have

been inspected by her and found to be in good order — and yet most of the food was missing?

'Josey, can you come here a minute?'

Josey came into the store room quickly. 'Yes, Mrs Parkington?'

'Can you tell me where all the stores are?'

The dinner lady gave the store room a quick examination and said, 'This is the way it normally is.'

Exasperated, Vera interrupted her, 'Yes, I can see there is a little of every rationed item here, but where are the stores?'

Josey shrugged her shoulders as she looked at Vera with a puzzled face. 'I dunno,' she said. 'Cook's in charge. She has the store key. I don't know where she keeps the new packets and that sort of thing.'

Vera knew immediately that something was amiss, but it was no use questioning Josey, who was only an assistant. Only the cook herself would know the answer.

A Helpful Friend

Vera was pleased to see Vic happily seated for his meal at a table with the youngest children. He seemed to have settled into school life like a duck to water — only she didn't want to think of water at the moment. She kept pushing any thoughts about water out of her mind.

'Mum,' announced Vic, whose face smiled when he saw her, 'Miss Smith says Penguin is getting drier on the radiator in her room, and I can have him when I go home.'

'That's very kind of her,' replied Vera, putting down a tray of jam tarts and custard on the table for the teacher to serve out to each child.

The children were seated at tables with a teacher at the head of each one to show them how to use the cutlery properly, and encourage them to converse as a social group, which Vera, as a School Meal Organiser, considered part of their education.

'Ooh!' exclaimed one little girl, 'we ain't had such nice dinner before, Miss. Corned beef fritters and mash to start, and then jam tarts for afters.'

'Mum's a good cook,' said Vic proudly.

'You're lucky,' another child told him.

It was a relief to hear that the children — and staff — appreciated the meal, but while she and Josey cleaned up the kitchen afterwards, her main worry entered her head again.

What am I going to do next?

She couldn't go to the baby-sitter's because the weather was still too bad. She couldn't afford a hotel, and hadn't anyone she knew who lived close enough to ask for accommodation.

The headmistress was up to her eyes dealing with parents who had come to collect their children early from school, and she had to wait to see her.

Vic was clearly very tired after this busy morning and sat with a still-damp Penguin in the school hall as it gradually emptied of children while the few remaining had Anne Driver on the radio listening to the *Music and Movement* programme for children. But the children were not paying attention, just looking out for someone to come and take them home.

At long last Miss Smith was free for Vera to approach. The lady had been very busy all day, but managed to smile at Vic and his mother.

'Ah, Mrs Parkington, and Victor Parkington — now what are we going to do with you?'

Vera was relieved that the headmistress seemed concerned about her plight, but it didn't seem to be the right moment to tell her that she suspected someone had been stealing the school food.

'The police have told me that the emergency services have set up a rescue centre for evacuees from the floods at

104

several places. There's one at an aerodrome and another one at the Women's Institute.'

'I think, as we have two dogs, the aerodrome would be best.'

'Good!' said Vic, 'I want to see some aeroplanes.'

So after what seemed like hours waiting around, they were picked up on a RAF truck and driven to the airfield. It was windy there, but they were safe.

There, the accommodation in a nissen hut was basic, but as Vera joined other bewildered, homeless people the wartime spirit of jollity and making do prevailed.

A stove in the centre of the hut was stoked with coal and gave some warmth. They were served hot drinks and sandwiches by kind, local volunteers, and after Vic had been washed in the bath hut and put to bed, with the dogs curled up by him, they were soon asleep.

But Vera sat on her narrow bed, hugged in a blanket, unable to sleep.

People had told her about their frightening experiences as the flood waters rose. And all the time more evacuees were arriving, although it was already night-time.

The stormy weather outside the hut made the windows rattle.

'I'm thinking of my poor chickens,' remarked the lady in the next bed.

But Vera was thinking of Geoff.

She felt sure he would not put himself in danger, but you never knew where the powerful force of flooding water would strike through a breach in a river bank. Battling against vicious winds would make the task of shoring up the weak places impossible for the workers to carry the sandbags up to the top of the banks.

In fact she'd been told by some of the evacuees that the workers had to give up trying in places . . . and water had topped the banks and spread quickly over the flat land.

Vera prayed Geoff would be safe. She had never known a time when she'd loved her husband more. She thought of his fragile state of mind and prayed he would be able to keep his nerve as well as do his job.

She also hoped he would realise that, although he couldn't speak to her, she would make sure she and Vic were out of danger.

A sudden shiver ran though her body, but was he all right?

* * *

At that moment Geoff wouldn't have described himself as being all right. So far, his river banks had held along the whole area he had been put in charge of. But he knew it was possible for a breach to occur because of the enormous pressure on them from the racing flood water.

He was cold, miserable, worried, and above all frightened for Vera and his son.

He'd seen Vera's car abandoned as he came towards Ely and had no idea where she was. She wasn't at the baby-sitter's house when he rang. Anyway, Enid Perrot's house down by the river-side was being flooded.

All day he'd been on edge because the telephone lines in places were down, and he hadn't had the time to ring Alice in case she now knew where Vera was.

Although, at the back of his mind, he was sure Vera, being a capable and sensible woman, would find somewhere safe to shelter. But he'd love to know for sure that she had, and that his little Vic was not scared out of his wits.

Because rescuing people from the floods was a priority, all the rescuers were so busy making sure people were safe that no lists had yet been made of those in the rescue centres.

Geoff knew he had to be patient. He'd done what he could to prevent flooding on his part of the river, but was alarmed as he observed the level continuing to rise. Especially when he was told the rivers were flooding in some areas and threatened disaster over large areas in the Fenlands.

Dickie Brightman, his assistant engineer, had offered him accommodation, but Geoff hadn't even had time to dump his things at his house. The weather forecast reported a hurricane and Geoff stayed up all night, waiting and watching.

When morning came it was strangely quiet after the storm. Vera had fallen asleep and was wakened by a damp, limp Penguin being thrust at her demanding some breakfast, and two dogs wanting to be let out.

'OK. I'll see what I can find,' Vera mumbled dreamily. Then, remembering where they were, she sat up and blinked. All the beds in the hut were occupied.

Scrambling into her clothes and making sure Vic was wrapped up against the cold they set of for the canteen. No-one seemed to mind the dogs, who were well behaved and sat with them while they had a cup of tea and a bowl of porridge.

'I don't like porridge,' said Vic, making a face.

'When you are in the forces you just have to put up with what you're given,' explained Vera, thinking the RAF cooks looked overworked.

There were many families in the big canteen, all looking dazed, and only the children seemed full of life and enjoying their unexpected holiday from school.

Vic soon made friends with two boys and the three of them were soon noisily zooming about, pretending to be planes, and annoying the other people at breakfast until they were told sharply by an RAF sergeant to go into a nearby hanger to play.

'I'd like to offer my help in the kitchen,' Vera said.

'Don't you worry about your boy,' said the mother of the two boys Vic was playing with, 'I'll keep an eye on him.'

'What about my dogs?'

'We have kennels for the RAF dogs,' said the sergeant. 'I'll ring the senior dog handler and he'll manage them.'

Vera didn't like to hand her dogs over to the strict routine the dogs had in kennels, but she knew they would be looked after — and they had to put up with the inconvenience this emergency had thrown at everyone.

Capped and gowned in kitchen wear, Vera was soon immersed in the work she knew so well: cooking for large numbers of people.

The RAF cooks soon recognised her abilities and before long Vera was being asked what to do.

'Well, we are not going to be short of food!' she remarked, looking at the huge food stores. But she knew only too well that having the ingredients was one thing — cooking them properly to make tasty meals was another.

Vera never dreamt that her first day working in the RAF canteen kitchen would be the first of many, because the Fen floods had only just begun, and many people were having to take refuge away from the flooded Fen areas.

It became a daily routine for her to

rise early to report to the canteen and start preparing breakfast for the people already sheltering at the station. Then it was a case of having food ready all day long for the new evacuees — a continuous buffet.

Being skilled at providing food for large numbers of people, Vera was soon accepted as being in charge of the catering, and was rushed off her feet every day.

Her young son was neglected by her, but fortunately seemed happy to be with the other children and knew she had to be in the kitchen all day to help feed everyone.

When Vic asked, 'Where's Dad?' she replied honestly that she didn't know, but added, 'He's very busy, I'm sure of that.'

'Can't he stop the water getting everywhere?'

Vera shook her head sadly, thinking of the harrowing tales people at the refuge had been reporting. 'No, Vic, he can't. Nor can anyone else. When the floods are over, then the engineers like him will have to see about preventing the dreadful flooding like this happening again.'

'It's not that dreadful being here,' declared Victor.

Vera stroked his hair gently, thinking he needed a hair cut — when was life going to be normal again?

Having Victor being looked after all day by some of the other women with children was a blessing. Vic seemed happy enough to be with a group of children of various ages.

Baby Peter was with her mother, and although she missed her baby and her dogs, she told herself she shouldn't worry about them — although she did of course.

And Geoff, she knew, would be very busy . . . she didn't like to think about what was happening to him. It was too painful. She just wished she knew.

Vera became friendly with another volunteer who came each day into the camp to help in the canteen. Isobel Browne was a sprightly older lady, whose husband was an RAF pilot and a senior officer in the station. Over a well-earned rest and cup of tea they often chatted.

One evening before returning to her sleeping hut, they were finishing a drink, when Isobel said, 'When Len leaves the RAF in a few months' time we are going to live in Scotland where our folks are.'

Vera thought of the Highlands with a sigh. 'I don't blame you getting away from these flat lands.'

'Oh, I wouldn't say we haven't liked being stationed here. The east coast has lots of attractions. We've enjoyed visiting the old cities like Norwich and Cambridge, and the charming old market towns. And the children love the beaches in the summertime. Any area has the potential for troubles — the winters in Scotland can be very cold and snowy.'

'You're right, of course. My folks live in Lynn so I want to stay here.'

Isobel took a drink of tea and sighed.

'This flooding is terrible — but exceptional. I'm sure the authorities will improve the flood defences now, after this disaster.'

'Yes,' agreed Vera, 'my husband has just started to work on that. He was in the Army during the war, and has only recently taken a job as a civil engineer here so he had hardly begun before this flooding happened . . . it has been . . . '

To her dismay Vera suddenly found she couldn't stop the tears from welling into her eyes and spilling down her cheeks.

She quickly wiped them away with her fingers, but the flow would not stop.

'I'm sorry,' sobbed Vera, 'I ought to pull myself together but I'm so worried about Geoff. I haven't heard from him . . . '

Isobel had put down her mug and leant forward studying Vera with a concerned expression. 'I can see you're exhausted, my dear. You've been slaving away here for over two weeks, night and day. You need a proper rest.'

'I'll be all right,' Vera replied with a heaving chest, determined to overcome her bout of crying, but it wouldn't go away.

Leaving Vera, Isobel slipped away and very soon a couple of RAF medical men were there to assist Vera back to her nissen hut.

'She's suffering from exhaustion,' declared the camp doctor.

'Well, she's not going to get any rest here,' declared Isobel looking around and seeing the camp hut was crowded and full of women and children.

'I'll take her to my house.'

Vera protested, 'You can't do that, Isobel. I have a young son and two dogs.'

'There's room for them all,' declared Isobel. 'I have two spare bedrooms now my children have left home.'

'Thank you,' Vera said lying on her bed, feeling unwilling to move, 'I'll find Victor and pack our things when I feel a bit better.'

It was obvious to Isobel that she

needed her help even to collect her belongings and to find her son — who seemed to be missing.

'He was being looked after by that family over there,' said Vera, sitting up and pointing to the noisy group at the far end of the hut.

'You stay where you are, Vera, I'll go and ask them where he is,' Isobel said.

But she came back after talking to them saying, 'They said they thought Vic was with you.'

A Frightening Time

Victor — where *was* Mrs Parkington's lost little boy?

Soon every mother in the hut was searching for him. Fearful that they might lose their own children they really felt sorry for Vera who they knew had been working hard at the canteen all day and even into the night-time, and had entrusted her child with them.

Weakened with work and worry, Vera sat on her bed with her head in her hands. She felt her sore eyes wanted to close and her feet didn't want to take her weight — but she must look for Victor.

'He was seen playing with some of the lads from another hut,' declared someone, 'I'll go over there and ask if they know where they are.'

She came back saying she'd spoken to two boys. 'They admitted they had been with Victor, goodness knows what they'd been up to — they looked distinctly embarrassed when I questioned them!'

Vera groaned. Boys, especially schoolboys, could get up to all kinds of trouble.

Isobel patted Vera's shoulder. 'Don't worry. Whatever they've done, my husband's the camp's Group Captain, and knows boys can be mischievous — especially as they are not at school at this difficult time.'

'Victor is only three,' Vera said, dabbing her watering eyes.

'Well, those boys are older,' said the woman with crossed arms who'd spoken to them. 'Most likely they've been doing something they shouldn't oughter.'

Vera head sank down and she closed her eyes. Maybe she should have kept Vic with her in the kitchen. But the child would have been bored cooped up in there.

Anyway, the women in the hut had assured her they would look after him — and she had been sure they had as

Victor had seemed quite happy being with the other children all day.

But now something had gone wrong.

Soon a massive hunt was going on to find her little boy. Even the camp tannoy was blaring out that a young boy, Victor Parkington, was missing, and would everyone on the camp look for him.

Time for Vera seemed to creep by slowly, as Isobel and some other women were busy filling Isobel's car with Vera's things.

'If you don't mind, we'll leave the dogs where they are and collect them another day,' Isobel suggested.

Vera nodded miserably. She got up and went out of the hut looking out at the darkening airfield.

'You'll catch your death standing there in that wind,' said one woman, offering her a blanket to wrap around her.

But Vera couldn't bring herself to move inside although she knew she might collapse with fatigue at any moment.

'Vic, where are you?' her voice would not sound as her eyes searched the darkening horizon.

Vera's strained face suddenly relaxed. She'd spied a familiar little figure running over the airfield, straight towards the hut — and into her arms.

She hugged him tight, realising he was crying, too.

Putting the blanket around his cold body, she steered him into the warmth of the hut.

There was a hush as mother and child entered, every eye on them.

Vera managed to croak, 'Thank you everyone for helping me. We're going to stay with Mrs Browne now . . . '

She heard many voices reply. 'Thank God you found him!'

'How is your boy?'

'Thank you, Vera, for giving us such good meals.'

'Goodbye.'

Isobel ushered Vera and Vic outside and into her waiting car.

Nestled up beside her on the back

121

seat, Victor told his mother that some older boys had taken Penguin from him and put his cuddly toy into a hut stove.

Vera knew that there was nothing she could do to bring back her child's security toy. He was having to learn a hard lesson in life.

'I went to the canteen to look for you — but you weren't there ... ' the distraught child sobbed.

As Vera comforted him, she felt the pain the boy was suffering. He was still little more than a baby, and had been wonderfully brave and cheerful during the emergency, and it seemed so cruel that Penguin had been needlessly destroyed.

All she could do was to hold him tight, kiss him, and wish it hadn't happened.

As Isobel drove out of the camp she stopped at the guard house and reported Victor Parkington had been found.

It was dark by the time they arrived at Isobel's home.

The house had no lights on and Isobel parked the car in the car port and then went to open the back door and switch on the kitchen light.

Vera blinked as she entered and felt the warmth of the Aga cooker, and approved of the cleanliness. Isobel told Vera to sit on one of the kitchen chairs while she went out to unload the car.

Vera wanted to assist Isobel, but felt too weak. She sank down on a chair, but Vic helped to carry some light things in.

'Thank you, Vic,' Isobel said, after they had strewn Vera's luggage around the kitchen, 'Now, it's a hot drink then a bath and bed for both of you.'

It was hard for Vera to get upstairs to a bedroom, but she longed to lie down.

Although Isobel was an older woman and had done a tiring day's work she was marvellous. Not only did she make sure her guests were bathed and tucked up in bed with a stone hot-water bottle, but she brought them a drink of Ovaltine.

To Vic's amazement, she produced a drawer of children's toys, which she said had belonged to her son and daughter, who were now grown up and had left home.

'I've been keeping them for my grandchildren,' she explained. 'But I'm sure they would be happy if you had one, Victor.'

Vic sat up in his bed and examined each one. 'I would really like this red Dinky toy car, Mrs Browne,' he said, looking at her hopefully.

'Then you shall have it.'

Penguin forgotten, Victor snuggled down to sleep with the little toy car parked beside him on his pillow.

'How can I ever thank you enough?' asked Vera.

'You don't have to, my dear,' said Isobel as she looked back at Vera lying in bed before she switched off her bedroom light and quietly closed the bedroom door.

Vera went to sleep immediately.

Geoff was overworked, too. He'd

been delighted to find his stretch of the river banks had held, but he'd travelled to another area that night where they had not been so fortunate.

Although some breaches in the banks along the river could not be prevented, some had been weakened and it was those areas that needed clay, willow and brushwood to strengthen the banks. Gangs of soldiers were striving to prevent further flooding as another gale battered the east coast.

Eventually, as the river water level ceased to rise, Geoff felt elated and that overcame his weakening physical strength. Like Vera he badly needed to rest. But he strove to keep his eyes open because his expertise was needed to tell the soldiers and other workers what to do, so he kept going.

When he heard the flood situation was finally under control, he struggled back to his car, but felt too exhausted to drive anywhere.

Later some soldiers found him asleep at the wheel. He was taken by ambulance to hospital where they diagnosed fatigue. He was not the only patient in there suffering from stress brought on by the horrendous flooding over the Fens.

★ ★ ★

Isobel Browne found Vic asleep with Vera in the morning. The little boy had woken up and, taking his red car, he'd gone into Vera's bedroom and snuggled down beside her.

She went downstairs to the kitchen again with Vera's untouched cup of tea, and said to her husband, Len, who was having his breakfast, 'Mother and child are still fast asleep.'

Len crunched his toast and marmalade and said, 'Best to leave them.'

Isobel sighed as she sat on a kitchen chair opposite Len. 'I know you are very busy up at the airfield, but if you could try and find out where Vera's husband is, I'm sure it would help Vera recover.'

Len looked over his glasses at his wife. 'Hmm. Have you any idea where he might be?'

Isobel shook her head and took a sip of her own tea. 'No . . . wait a moment. She said he was working on the river banks — strengthening them.'

Len remarked dryly, 'Together with hundreds of soldiers, local men and prisoners of war!'

'Oh, I know it is like looking for a needle in a hay stack — but Vera did say he was one of the river engineers.'

Len finished his cup of tea and smacked his lips as he rose to his feet. 'Well, you'll be pleased to hear the worst of the flooding is now over and the pumping of the flooded Fen areas will begin. So gradually everyone caught up in this tragedy will begin to sort themselves out. There should be some lists available of where people are. I'll get in touch with Military Headquarters and mention his name . . . what is it?'

'Parkington. Geoffrey, I think Vera

said he was. Colonel Parkington of the Royal Engineers, during the war.'

'Oh, that chap who helped design Mulberry.'

Isobel was impressed Len had heard of him. 'She didn't tell me about that.'

Picking up his briefcase, Len strode out the kitchen. 'I'll see what I can do to locate him. Now you're not to go to the camp canteen today. Stay here and look after our guests.'

'Yes, sir,' said Isobel with a slight smile and a mock salute.

A Plea For Help

Vera recovered rapidly, and was soon up and about helping Isobel — who had taken on her, and her young son, as guests.

'Does your husband mind us being here?' Vera asked Isobel on the second day at the Browne's home, coming downstairs for breakfast after hearing Len drive away in his car. She didn't want to get in the way of their early morning routine so had stayed in her room until he'd departed.

'No, of course not. You're no trouble, my dear.'

'I wouldn't say that, having a three-year-old in the house to look after.'

Isobel smiled. 'I'm used to children, and Victor is no trouble. Although I expect he might be getting a little bored being here without any other children to play with. Now, sit down and help yourself to cereal while I make a pot of tea. I have some good news for you.'

Vera caught Isobel's arm and stared questioningly into her eyes, 'Have you heard where Geoff is?'

'Len heard he's in a military hospital.'

Vera's face paled. 'Is he all right?'

'Well, we don't know why he is there — but Len was told he is not on the danger list. So don't look so worried, Vera, I'm sure he'll soon be as right as rain.'

As the kettle whistle began to sound, and steam puffed out, Isobel went over to the Aga to make the tea.

As Vera began her breakfast she explained how Geoff had suffered during the war. She said he'd been invalided out because of his unstable mental state after being injured by a bomb exploding near him. 'You see why I'm really scared, Isobel. He might have had another breakdown . . . ' Tears welled into her eyes.

But Isobel's answer to that was brisk.

'Relax Vera, eat your breakfast, you are still recovering yourself.'

'No, no — I'm fine.'

'You're not. You wouldn't be crying if you were fully recovered. Imagining your husband is in all sorts of trouble when you don't know all the facts is just looking for worry! I would guess, from what Len told me, that Geoff has been overworking in the last few weeks, lacking sleep, just as you were.'

Vera smiled though her tears. 'I hope you're right.'

'Now, let's concern ourselves with what we are going to have to eat for lunch and for dinner when Len comes in. You're an expert cook, so he will expect a good meal. Won't he?'

Vera, had to agree and to take Isobel's advice to push out of her mind her worries about Geoff. They had to think about shopping and cooking which was much more agreeable for her. And her little boy, 'Where's Vic?' she asked.

'Out in the garden, on the swing that was put up for my children.'

'He'll love that,' declared Vera. 'He likes to be active. In fact I was wondering if Miss Smith, the headmistress of Roundwood School, would allow him to be a temporary pupil while we are staying in Ely. I'll have to find us board and lodging here for awhile.'

'You can stay here as long as you like,'

'That won't be fair on you, besides I have the dogs.'

'Now listen, my dear. This house is big enough for you all. You, your husband, children — and dogs.'

Vera chuckled. 'I know it is — it's a lovely house, but that isn't fair on you to have us all here.'

Isobel smiled. 'So, Len and I will be invaded. But he won't mind I'm sure. He's much too busy. There's a huge military operation being prepared to start draining the Fenlands. The Dutch, who have low-lying lands like us, are sending us some of their pumps and the whole business takes a lot of organising.'

Vera could imagine the work involved,

and she did want to stay with Isobel but she asked her, 'Why should you put yourself out for us?'

'Because this is an emergency, like wartime, when we had evacuees. And you are in need of a home.'

Vera sighed. What Isobel said was true. She did need a place to stay until she could get to her mother's. 'Just for a few days then. I'd be grateful.'

'Well, I'd be grateful if you cook for us — I'm a hopeless cook.'

'Of course I will,' Vera retorted, and sighed with relief.

Vera hadn't been as concerned about baby Pete, because she knew he was safely with her mother, but it wasn't long before that part of her family came into her mind.

'Are the telephone lines repaired, do you know, Isobel? I'd like to speak to my mother.'

'Yes, do ring her. The telephone is in the hall.'

It was when Vera got through to her mother on a rather crackly line that she felt immensely better. Her mother had a soothing effect on Vera's nerves, assuring her that they were all well and that there had been no flooding where she was — and the baby was thriving.

However, she didn't advise Vera to come to Lynn yet as she didn't know if the roads were safe to travel on with trees down.

'I can't anyway, 'Vera said. 'I haven't a car.'

'Oh dear, what happened to it?'

'I have no idea. I had to abandon it at the side of the road. But that's the least of my worries — Geoff is . . . ' Vera's voice died.

'How's he?' asked Alice.

Vera took a deep breath. 'In hospital,' replied Vera flatly.

Waiting to hear more, Alice said nothing.

Vera gulped, trying to overcome her distress, then said, 'I only know that he's in hospital.'

Alice was her usual cheerful self. 'I'm sure he's being well taken care of.'

The front door bell rang and Vera had to hurriedly say goodbye to her mum, because it wasn't her house and Isobel may have a visitor at the door she may want to show into her sitting-room. But she heard the visitor talking to Isobel by the front door for a while.

'Someone to see you,' called Isobel, and Margaret, looking well-dressed and confident as she peeled off her leather gloves, removed her hat, smiled briefly at Vera as she walked past her into the sitting-room where she sat down without being asked.

Vera followed her, wishing she'd made a little more effort with her appearance that morning. She was still in her slippers as she observed Margaret's polished court shoes.

'Hello, Vera. Crumbs, you do look washed out,' Margaret remarked, studying her friend.

However, Vera was not going to be put down by Margaret. 'I dare say I do,' she replied tartly. 'I've been providing food for the five thousand in the last few weeks — while you've been sitting in your office at the Town Hall.'

Margaret smiled wryly. 'Yes, it wasn't fair of me to criticise you — I've heard so much praise about your work up at the airfield.'

'Did you?' asked Vera, surprised.

Margaret chuckled, 'I should say. So many people have told me that they appreciated your meals there.'

Vera shrugged, 'I did my best — there was plenty of food stored up there so it was easy.'

'Talking about stores,' said Margaret, 'that's why I came.'

'I gather it wasn't to commiserate with my health.'

Margaret laughed. 'That, too.'

Vera grinned. 'Well, as you can see I've survived. But I have no home or car, as I had to abandon it on the flooded road. My husband is in hospital and I'm worried about him . . . ' she sighed as she went on to say, 'Baby Peter is with my mother. My dogs are in kennels they won't like. And Victor's beloved toy penguin was taken from him by some bully boys and destroyed — so when you see him, please don't ask where his penguin is. Apart from all that, I suppose you could say, I'm OK.'

Margaret looked at Vera with sympathy. 'I am sorry you've had a rough time and Victor, too, it seems.'

'Oh, Vic is all right. He's outside in the garden, 'Vera's eyes went towards the window to see if she could see him.

Margaret got up to look. 'I see he's growing fast.'

'He certainly is.'

'I've been doing your job while you are not able to. I have several schools to visit today.'

Isobel knocked on the door and brought them in a cup of coffee. 'I thought you'd like a drink after your long drive from Norwich,' she said, placing the tray on a small table near Margaret.

'Isobel has been so kind to us,' remarked Vera.

Margaret nodded. 'I understand

you'll be staying here for a while, Vera.'

'Yes, she will,' answered Isobel quickly before Vera could reply. 'She'll be here until she has put her life together again.'

'Most kind,' murmured Vera.

Isobel said, 'It's to my advantage, I assure you. Gaining a great cook and companion.' With that comment Isobel smiled and left the room.

Margaret took a cup of coffee, sipped it and shifted herself on her chair.

'Actually, I came partly to ask you a favour, Vera.'

Vera pressed her lips together but gave a chuckle. 'You don't say! I haven't anything to give you. Anyway, go ahead. Ask away.'

'It has been reported to my office that Roundwood School here in Ely needs a cook temporarily. To replace the previous one who was found to be taking some food from the stores to sell on the black market.'

'You heard that I was there for one day?' asked Vera.

'Yes, Headmistress told me the school had loved your cooking.'

'Who told you about the missing stores?'

'Miss Smith told me the dinner lady, Josey Willow, mentioned it to her because she was afraid she might be accused of stealing it. I gather Josey isn't managing very well on her own . . . so I wondered if you would help out until another cook is appointed? Just for a week or two?'

Vera was stunned for a moment. Then she remembered how Miss Smith had helped her when she'd arrived that day all soggy wet, with piles of luggage, a child and two dogs.

She took a deep breath. 'Well, I suppose could I go there while I'm staying here. I can't do my job without my car, which is missing. It isn't far to walk to Roundwood from here. I had in mind to ask Miss Smith if she'd take Vic in her nursery class — he has no-one to play with.'

'Right!' declared Margaret. She got

up and walked into the hall where she replaced her hat and gloves and strode towards the front door. 'Thank you, Vera. I'll find another assistant to help Josey with the ordinary kitchen work; but when you feel well enough if you can manage to go there and suggest some meals for them to make, and replace the store cupboard, it would be a help. Goodbye.'

'Hold on. I want to ask you a favour.'

Margaret paused, holding the door open to leave, with eyebrows raised questioningly as she looked back at Vera.

'Please visit Geoff. See how he is, and let me know.'

'Right, I'll do that.'

Vera knew that Geoff had known Margaret before she'd met him, and he had helped her when she'd needed support as a widowed mother before the war.

Vera continued, 'And would you be kind enough to go up to the airfield and get my dogs from the kennels — and bring them here?'

Margaret laughed. 'That's two favours!'

'I have one more, Margaret. Please find my car.'

'I'd better go, in case you think of anymore.' But as Margaret went out she popped her head around the door, saying, 'I'll see what I can do. Look after yourself.'

Vera went back into the sitting-room and lay back in the armchair, and sighed.

Her venture — her new life — had fallen to bits, but she was fortunate to have good people around her helping her. She now had to mend it.

A Dream Come True

Always on her mind, but thoughts of Geoff had to be shelved, so Vera got on with her life as best she could. She'd had to do it before when Geoff was in the Army during the war and when he'd been injured and in hospital.

Missing her baby, Peter, was hard to bear. How was her mother getting on with looking after him? Mum said she was managing, but it couldn't be easy for her to have a lively baby to look after at her age . . .

Getting back to work was one way to cope with her longing to be with them again.

Isobel and Len showed great kindness in giving her and her son a home. She explained her troubles to them that evening. 'I really don't know what to do, I've been asked to work at Roundwood School for a few weeks because not having a car means I can't do my normal job. Nor will I be able to go to my mum's house in Lynn without transport. And heaven knows what has happened to the cottage we were living in . . . flooded I'm sure. Then I ought to go and see how Geoff is . . . '

Vera daren't go on, feeling she might burst into tears.

Isobel looked at Len saying, 'We have discussed your situation, my dear, and we are happy for you to stay here for as long as you like.'

'But that's putting an enormous burden on you,' protested Vera.

Len said in his officer-in-charge voice, 'Let's take one thing as a time, shall we? First, you really must not worry about us having you here. We wouldn't have asked you to stay if you were, 'a burden', as you put it. Isn't that right, Isobel?'

Isobel nodded in agreement saying, 'Just accept our hospitality knowing that you would do the same for anyone in an emergency. Wouldn't you?'

Vera grinned. 'I doubt if I would have your patience. Thank you so much.'

Len continued, 'So now to the next thing. I'll drive you over to the hospital to see your husband on Sunday when I'm having a day off duty. In the meantime, if you feel up to it, you can go to the school and help there. Then perhaps your step-father and mother can bring the baby over here? I'll check the road is in use again.'

Vera almost cried, 'Oh, thank you!'

'And finally, your animals are still languishing in kennels. Miss Smallwood told me that she'd made enquires and found out that your two dogs were transferred to the RSPCA kennels with many of the other dogs lost in the floods. The RSPCA will be only too glad to get them back to their owners, so I'll run over there to reclaim them for you if you like?'

This time Vera couldn't stop her tears from falling. 'Sorry,' sobbed Vera. 'You are both so kind.'

'She's tired,' said Isobel. 'Go to bed, my dear.'

★ ★ ★

When morning came, Vera felt she was a different person. She had regained some of her energy and optimism, and felt like a person who'd gone through a difficult patch in life and was now about to start afresh. Her problems seemed manageable.

After breakfast she rang the headmistress of Roundwood and said she would come in and help Josey in the kitchen.

'Good,' exclaimed Miss Smith. 'She's in a right dither. I thought I'd have to go and help her prepare the lunch.'

Vera giggled at the thought. The school was still recovering from the effects of the emergency so she asked, 'I was wondering if you would allow me to bring Victor, as he is alone all day with no other children here.'

'Of course, bring Victor. He can be put in the kindergarten class.'

'One other thing — '

'Yes?'

'During our stay at the airfield with the other evacuees, some bigger boys bullied Vic and took his comfort toy penguin and threw it into a camp stove.'

'Dear me!'

'Anyway, Vic has got over it now because he was given a toy car.'

'Splendid! But don't allow him to bring it here.'

Vera was glad Vic liked the idea of being a schoolboy. He agreed to leave his Dinky car parked on his bedroom window-sill and trotted off happily to the school he knew.

Miss Smith was busy, but seemed very welcoming and when Vera got to the school kitchen she knew why. The place seemed to be disorganised. Assistant cook, Josey Willow, was flustered and on the point of abandoning the work and going home.

Vera put her arm around the young woman and told her, 'Please don't go.

We can sort things out. Now make us a cup of tea while I wash my hands, then we can see about feeding the children.'

Josey smiled through her tears.

Sitting at the kitchen table and discussing what was possible to prepare with few food items available, was a problem Vera was used to facing.

During her working life she had run a British Restaurant with wartime rations — and cooked meals in France just before D-Day with whatever food she could find for many people to eat.

Now, so soon after the war, food rations were still difficult for any cook.

Josey's round face lost its look of despair as they agreed to bake some large potatoes. Then to fill them they could grate some cheese, and carrot. For afters, Vera thought it might be fun for the children to make some ginger-bread men to go with a semolina pudding.

'How do you do that?' Josey asked, wide-eyed.

'We'll start by making a biscuit

dough. You know how to do that don't you?'

Josey nodded. 'If you tell how much flour and marge and sugar to mix.'

'You'll need to add a little bicarbonate of soda, mixed spice and ground ginger, too. I'll show you exactly how much.'

Having cleaned the potatoes and put them in the oven, the two dinner ladies then started the rather fiddly job of rolling out the biscuit mix and making oblong shapes for the bodies, a blob rolled then flattened for the head, and thin strips for the arms and legs which they attached with a little dried egg mixture.

Josey was put to work putting currants on the faces for the eyes, while Vera checked the time, and warmed another oven to a moderate heat for the biscuits.

The semolina was measured out and added to some milk and sugar, put in basins and put in the oven, too.

'All done,' Vera said, dusting the flour

from her hands, and Josey beamed at her.

★ ★ ★

'The gingerbread men went down a treat,' said Josey after the meal as she wheeled in the trolley laden with clattering empty dishes to be washed.

Vera felt pleased to see Josey looking radiant. It had only taken a little know-how and encouragement. Vera smiled at her hardworking and caring assistant, but felt very tired, because she knew her job was not yet finished.

She still had to decide on what to make for meals for the next few school days — and order the missing store cupboard items for Margaret to bring.

After all was done, Vera went to collect her little son, who seemed subdued, and with plasters on his cheek and knee.

'Vic has had a good day,' said the nursery teacher. 'He learns very quickly and we did a few sums, didn't we, Vic?'

Vic nodded.

'He liked the story I read to the class, didn't you, Vic?'

Vic nodded.

'In the playground he learned to play hopscotch — and he had a scrap with another boy, so he's now tired out. He's not used to a full day at school, Mrs Parkington. He may like to stay at home tomorrow and come in another day?'

'No,' said Vic, 'I want to go to school every day.'

'We'll see,' Vera said, taking his small hand to leave. 'Thank you.'

'And thank you for the enjoyable school dinner, Mrs Parkington. The children loved the gingerbread men.'

Feeling very satisfied Vera began walking back to Isobel's house with Vic chattering non-stop, thinking it seemed a long way. Even Vic's little legs seemed to drag and Vera wondered if she might collapse before they got there.

Suddenly she became aware that a car had drawn up beside them. The driver had opened the window — it was Margaret.

'Hello, Vera. I went to collect you from school but was told you had just left.'

There was someone else in the car besides Margaret and Vera staggered when the passenger door opened — and out got Geoff.

'My darling!' he said as his eyes caught hers and he smiled, then with a few strides he took Vera in his strong arms.

Oblivious to their surroundings they held each other kissing and hugging. Vic demanded, and received, his father's fond attention, too, in the joyful reunion.

Vera no longer felt exhausted as she clung to Geoff, being assured that he was well.

Margaret in the meantime separated Vic and put him into the car shouting, 'I'll leave you two to saunter back.' And with that she drove off and left the lovers together.

They had a party when Vera and

Geoff arrived back at the house. Isobel welcomed Geoff in the same kindly way Vera had been welcomed into her home.

The last to arrive was Len — and a carload of tail-wagging dogs.

Gyp was wild with excitement to be reunited with his family as they were to see him, but old Battle was only able to trot about and lick everyone before he flopped down by Geoff's armchair.

Margaret said she had to leave to collect her small daughter, Deanna.

'Thanks ever so much, Margaret, for all you've done to help me,' said Vera, seeing her off.

'I've still got to find your car,' said Margaret, waving goodbye.

Vera shouted at her as she drove off, 'Thanks again, Margaret.'

Vera stood watching until the car disappeared at the end of the road, thinking that owing to the goodness and kindness of people, her family were all together again — except for baby Peter, and Vera hoped he would be

She found Isobel in her dressing-gown already down in the kitchen making tea for everyone.

Isobel said, 'Good morning, Vera. Len has taken the dogs out for a short walk. He didn't want to disturb Geoffrey, who is still asleep.'

Vera thanked her but had another question burning her. 'Isobel,' she said, 'You are both so kind. But are you and Len sure about letting us buy this house?'

Isobel took the steaming kettle from the Aga and poured the water into the warmed tea pot saying, 'Of course we are sure. Don't imagine we didn't think about the transaction carefully before we offered the house to you and Geoffrey. It will benefit us, too. It saves us having to find a buyer and having the house agent fees. We thought not many people will be wanting to move to Ely after the Fen floods — although you are perfectly safe living here on a hill.'

Vera helped her put out the mugs for tea, and poured a little milk into them.

joining them soon.

Anyway, they were all safe and unharmed. Vera said a prayer of thanks as she went into the kitchen to prepare a simple meal for everyone.

But after having fed everyone and the dogs, and taken Vic, her tired little schoolboy, upstairs to bed she had to struggle to go downstairs again — she felt almost too exhausted.

However, she was glad she did. There was some exciting news waiting for her.

Snuggled up by Geoff on the sofa she listened to the wonderful news he told her, 'Len and Isobel are planning to move to Scotland and have offered us their house.'

Vera blinked. 'We haven't enough money . . . '

'I have discussed a repayment plan with your husband, Vera,' interrupted Len.

'Yes,' Geoff explained, 'it will be a private sale. We will pay for the house as and when we can. It is most generous of Isobel and Len to do this for us.'

Stunned, Vera hands went over her cheeks, her eyes sparkling with joy as she thanked them. It was almost unbelievable — yet it was true — she was to have her dream home.

Isobel and Len looked at each other, clearly happy with the arrangement.

Suddenly the door opened and Vic in his pyjamas appeared, struggling as he carried his father's violin case. 'Dad,' the small boy said sleepily, 'I came to give you your violin — I saved it from the floods.'

Geoff got up immediately and, picking Vic up in his strong arms, he thanked him, kissed him, then he took him back upstairs to bed.

Concerns About Geoff

When morning came Vera had regained her strength. Although Geoff was in the other single bedroom she felt a wave of happiness to know he was with her again. But she couldn't stay in bed for long as another busy day loomed before her.

'To think this house will soon be our new home,' she kept muttering to herself and smiling as she got washed and dressed. It was delightful just to have the thought mulling in her mind.

She slipped into Geoff's room, saw he was sleeping, and gave him a light kiss so as not to wake him. She wanted to stay there. But she knew she must get on and concentrate on another busy day ahead, as Josey needed her in the school kitchen to advise and help with the food preparation.

'I can't begin to thank you enough,' she said.

'We know you are both delighted to have the house, my dear. It will be your first home and suitable for your family. It is a strange thing but when you leave a house you've enjoyed living in, as Len and I have, we like to think we are putting it into safe hands. And we think you, Geoffrey, and your children are the kind of people who will treasure it, too. And you deserve it.'

Vera would have thanked her again but the back door opened and in burst Gyp followed by lumbering Battle, while Len hung up their dog leads.

'Good morning!' Len said, looking hale and hearty after his walk. 'I'm surprised to see you up and about, Vera. You looked as if you would sleep for a week last night.'

Vera smiled at the older man. 'I felt like it. But I have to get up to the school this morning and make sure the children are fed properly. The cook has been dismissed for thieving, and the one assistant is not trained and can just about open a can of Spam, although I'm hoping to get her into a cookery class, as I think she'll be fine when she knows what to do.'

Len grabbed a mug of tea saying, 'I must report for duty, too. The airfield needs bringing back into order now that the last of the refugees have left. And we are shorthanded so I'll need to roll up my sleeves and do a bit of clearing up, too.'

'I wanted to thank you,' began Vera.

'No need,' said Len, 'the arrangement will suit us both. Good luck to you and your young family.' He quickly drank his tea, plonked his empty mug by the sink, and kissed Isobel, saying, 'I'll see you later.' Then, picking up his cap and briefcase, he left the two women getting the breakfast while the dogs slurped water and settled down to sleep by the warm Aga.

Eating their cereal, the women were discussing the packing facing Isobel, when Vic came into the kitchen, fully dressed, but with uncombed, tousled hair, announcing that he was intending to go to school.

'OK,' said Vera, thinking Isobel would appreciate not having a lively young boy around as she planned her packing. 'Go and fetch your brush and comb, you can't go to school looking as if you've just crawled out of bed.'

When the boy had gone, Vera sipped her tea, and said to Isobel, 'I wish I had more clothes for Vic — his shorts and jersey badly need a wash but he hasn't any to change into.'

The same applied to her. She needed a fresh blouse and skirt. She explained, 'I only had room in the car to take one suitcase of underwear before we left the cottage. I hurriedly stuffed all sorts of bags into the car, but a lot of it I don't need now. Perhaps Geoff will be able to get over to the cottage at the weekend.'

But of course she knew Geoff had enough on his plate with his work to think about. She shouldn't really ask him — not yet anyway. And buying new clothes was an expense they didn't need right now.

Isobel said, 'I'm sure the teachers will understand some children's parents are finding it difficult to dress their children. Ask Margaret if the county council have a fund to help families like you.'

'That's a good idea. I will. I may be able to get some school wear for Vic.'

'And I dare say as I clear out my drawers to pack I'll find some old clothes we don't want that might be useful for you and Geoffrey.'

There was no time for Vera to repeat her heartfelt thanks — she had to think of getting Vic to school on time.

★   ★   ★

The first thing Vera noticed as she approached the school was a van marked with *School Meal Service* on its side.

'Bless you, Margaret,' she breathed, knowing her supplies had come.

Josey was busy telling the driver where to put the boxes of stores and once again Vera had the feeling she would make a good cook. Her enthusiasm for her job was clear, and with the training Vera could give her, plus cookery classes, she would soon turn into a competent cook.

It was a weight off Vera's mind. Although, at present she had to act as the cook — and teach Josey at the same time.

The day in the school kitchen raced by.

The headmistress popped into the kitchen with Vic before Vera went home, and Vera thought for one awful moment her little boy was in trouble. But the head only came to say how much the school had enjoyed the dish of mince, pasta and cheese following by the chocolate pudding the two cooks had made.

'Thanks,' Vera said, taking off her overall.

'Vic's teacher thought he'd had

enough for one day, so I've brought him along for you to take him home.'

'Yes, his father came home last night and he stayed up rather late.'

'Vic told me — '

'Actually, I was going to ask you if Vic can join the school, because we will be living here in future.'

Miss Smith looked surprised and Vera told her about the good news she'd heard last night.

'Well, that's splendid!'

Vera pressed on, 'I doubt if my baby-sitter will be able to cope with Vic, as he is used to school life now. Will you enrol him — he's almost four years old?'

Miss Smith smiled at Vera and then down at Vic. 'Well these are unusual times, and you have helped our school, so I will see what can be done. Your son has fitted into the nursery class very well, the teacher tells me.'

Another weight came off Vera's shoulders as she was sure Victor would be given a place and she would be able to get on with her regular job.

When she arrived home, her happiness was complete as her mother and step-father had arrived with baby Pete.

Vera was sure no-one in the world could be happier than she was holding her baby in her arms again. And my goodness how he'd grown!

'You'll be toddling around soon, getting into mischief,' she said, cuddling him.

There was a great deal for the family to catch up on.

Vera's mum told her how lucky she was to be getting Isobel and Len's lovely house.

'You don't have to tell me, Mum,' Vera said, kissing her, 'I'm over the moon!'

But as the days went by, practical problems arose.

When Isobel began sorting out her things to leave, it suddenly hit Vera that her house would be left empty when the Brownes left.

'Geoff,' she said, 'when Isobel and

Len go, there'll be nothing left in the house. No beds or furniture — and how can I cook with no cookware?'

Geoffrey Parkington had resumed his job as a river engineer, and was very busy after the floods. Vera didn't want to bother him about the problem of the house being empty — but she had to ask if they could go back to their cottage in the Fens and salvage what they could.

Vera dismissed from her mind that she thought Geoff looked worried at times. She was so busy herself, she didn't think much about it, but the niggle persisted.

On a Saturday morning Geoff had to go to work, as was the custom with most workers after the war, so he couldn't take her over to the cottage until the afternoon and they arranged for the children to be looked after.

The long straight roads they drove along through the Fenlands towards where they used to live showed the land had been underwater. In some places pools of water remained.

'It all looks so bleak,' remarked Vera, as she saw that many trees had come down and the trunks had been moved to the side of the road.

'Fortunately, the Fenland is very fertile, and the farmers will soon make it fine agricultural land again.'

'But just look at that farm!' Vera said, pointing ahead.

The devastation was clearly visible. Heartbreaking for the farmer to have his window broken and the door of his house hanging off — and his farm buildings torn down by surging water crashing into them whipped up by the strong winds.

Vera wondered what would be left of their cottage.

It was still there when they arrived, but the little cottage had obviously been damaged by the flood waters surging around it, although the water had drained away.

They parked the car and went to examine the property.

'Look, the water's flooded the ground floor.'

Vera had to press her lips together tightly. All her household belongings — her family's clothes, furniture and pot and pans, would have been submerged or partly submerged by water. And as most of their things had been stored downstairs all would have been ruined or washed away.

She felt Geoff take her hand and squeeze it. 'I'm sorry,' he said.

'It's not your fault,' she said with tears in her eyes. 'We'll just have to manage somehow. Mum can lend me some things.'

'I feel guilty bringing you here in the first place.'

'Don't say that, Geoff. It was the best thing to do at the time — and you didn't know about the floods at the time. Nobody expected the tragedy. Anyway, we are safe, the children are unhurt and we have a wonderful house that we wouldn't have had if the floods hadn't driven us away from here.'

Geoff swallowed. 'That is true. But, well, I just hope things will work out.'

Vera frowned. That was the second hint she'd had that Geoff was worried about something. Was it that he didn't think he would ever be able to pay for the house? Or was he suffering from something and he wasn't telling her about it?

'Anyway, now we're here, we'd better see if there is anything upstairs that is worth saving.'

Their guess that the place had been gutted was true. Vera picked up a few items that she felt she could use. Some objects on higher shelves and at the top of cupboards she took to the car. However, very few undamaged items of their family belongings remained — not that they had many in the first place.

'Perhaps there's some clothes and bedding upstairs,' said Vera looking around her in dismay. 'I could take some clothes to wash — I badly need some, so do you and the children.'

The ladder to get upstairs was

missing, Geoff and Vera had to move some of the water-ruined furniture so he could stand on it and haul himself up to look around up there.

'Ugh!' she heard him exclaim and she did not have to ask him why as a large rat jumped down from above and scurried passed her feet, followed by another — and another.

Vera screamed. The upstairs had become rat infested!

Geoff almost jumped down, and putting his arm around Vera's shoulders, he ushered her out to the car. 'I don't think you'd want anything from up there,' he said, opening the car door so she could sit inside.

She was trembling.

She breathed deeply as she took her hankie to wipe her tears.

Vera looked at Geoff's face and didn't have to be told he detested rats. She was thankful she hadn't brought Vic with them to collect some of his toys.

Telling Len and Isobel about their horrid find that evening, they joked about the rats moving in.

'Well, my dear,' Isobel said to Vera, 'There are lots of things here we won't want to take with us. The carpets and furniture are well worn after we and our children have had it for years. My kitchen ware is very old and I look forward to buying new things as the wartime rationing is easing.'

'We will pay for anything you don't want,' Vera assured her.

'I assure you what we leave behind would go to the rag and bone man. So if you can make use of anything I don't want to take with us, that's fine by me.'

Once again Vera felt like crying. Len and Isobel's kindness and generosity was overwhelming. She told Geoff and he agreed that they had been exceptionally lucky to have met the couple.

Geoff said, 'People usually like to help others if they can. So don't worry about having what they offer you, Vera. I'm quite sure Isobel wouldn't be showering you with things you need if she wanted them for herself. Len and Isobel are not daft. They are keen to start a new life up in Scotland. They will have their family there so won't be without help themselves.'

Vera drank in Geoff's words. He was right, of course. She should just be thankful that all would be well in the future.

And yet, was it?

If only she could find out what was giving Geoff sleepless nights — because although they had to sleep in separate rooms until Len and Isobel left and they could use their double bed, Vera was sure she'd awoken some nights and heard Geoff wandering around downstairs.

What was it that was making him unable to sleep?

The Truth

It was weeks later before Vera's life settled into a normal pattern, and all the worries and fears she'd suffered during the river flood slipped into her unconsciousness.

'I keep pinching myself each morning that we own this beautiful house,' she told Geoff as they got dressed the day after Isobel and Len left for Scotland.

'We haven't paid for it yet,' Geoff reminded her, pausing as he shaved.

Vera badly needed new clothes for herself and the children, but she dare not mention that as every penny was needed to pay their huge debt. She had to make and mend just as they did during the war.

'How long will it take us to pay back Len and Isobel?'

Geoff continued to shave, not answering her, so Vera put the question to him again. 'As you know I'd love to have another child — so how long must we wait before we can afford for me to give up work?'

'I don't know, Vera. I just don't know, so please don't pester me about it now.'

Vera, who was rolling her nylons up her legs, trying to get the seam on the back straight, stopped to stare at Geoff. 'Is your work becoming too much for you?'

Dabbing his face with a towel and throwing it down on the bed before picking up his shirt, slipping into it and buttoning it up and then taking his tie, he proceeded to put it on while Vera looked at him, puzzled.

She'd been so busy with her job and the boys to look after — and settling into their new home. Perhaps, she hadn't noticed that Geoff hadn't been quite as content as she'd been?

'Geoffrey Parkington,' she commanded. 'Please tell me what's wrong with you.'

With his hands still tying a knot in his tie, Geoff turned to look at her anxious eyes. 'It's nothing you can help me with, Vera. Just something I've got to battle with myself.'

Vera felt dismayed. She'd thought all their troubles were over, and yet clearly her beloved Geoff was still fighting with some demon. 'What is it, Geoff?'

Dressed and ready for work, he hesitated before leaving the bedroom. 'I have to take the dogs for a quick walk so I can't talk about it now,' he said brusquely, and left the room.

Brushing her hair, Vera, too, had to go and dress the boys, get breakfast for everyone, take Vic to school, and Pete to the baby-sitter, before reporting for work herself. Her life couldn't be busier. Yet, having Geoff bothered by something, well, that added to the load of responsibilities she carried with her.

She couldn't ask him about it as he was already thumping down the stairs and the dogs were at the bottom with wagging tails waiting for their early-morning exercise.

Vera sighed. Maybe she shouldn't

have mentioned about her longing to have another child. She would dearly like a baby girl. Or maybe it was just the wrong time to have brought up the subject of increasing their family?

She sighed again. She'd got over many difficulties in her life, and yet the latest blow seemed almost worse that any she'd suffered previously. Was Geoff unable to cope with his job? Was he going to be dismissed? And what would happen to her lovely home if he was? She couldn't afford to pay for it on her low salary.

'Mum! Mum!' she could hear Vic shouting, 'I've lost a sock.'

Sighing once again, Vera came out of her reverie and became aware of the hundred-and-one things she had to do that day.

'Coming,' she shouted back as she checked in the mirror to see if she was properly dressed before leaving the bedroom, and hoping she had enough eggs in the pantry for breakfast for the family.

Later that day, when Vera met Margaret after inspecting a school's kitchen, they sat in Vera's car for a chat.

'I detect something isn't quite right?' said Margaret. 'I thought the kitchen here was first class, and the cook seems a competent woman.'

'Yes,' agreed Vera.

'So? You're the expert cook — what did she do wrong?'

Vera replied with a little laugh. 'Nothing. She does a good job — better than most. I usually find something like a dirty dish cloth or some mouldy cheese in the pantry — but this kitchen gets full marks from me.'

'So, what's eating you?'

Vera looked away from Margaret's searching eyes. 'I don't know . . . '

'What do you mean? You don't know!'

Vera looked down as she rubbed her hands together nervously, 'It's nothing to do with this kitchen — or with my job.'

'For goodness' sake, tell me,' Margaret's bossy nature come to the fore. 'I haven't all day to sit here. I must get back to the office as I have a pile of reports to write.'

Vera gave a great sigh, and said, 'Geoff isn't happy.'

Margaret knew Geoff well and looked immediately concerned. 'Trouble between you?' she asked.

'No. Not really.'

'Then what? For heaven's sake.'

'He won't tell me, that's the trouble. But I have the feeling he might be worried about paying for the house.'

Margaret sat quietly for a moment, then said, 'Well, it's going to take some time for you and Geoff to pay it off, but with two of you working it shouldn't be impossible.'

'Unless Geoff has another breakdown — he looks so worried.'

'Well, after the river floods he's bound to have a great deal of work to do.'

Vera retorted, 'His river banks held.'

The two women looked at each other, until Margaret said, 'Then it must be something else. Ask him again. I must go. Keep me informed about Geoff — I'm just as concerned about him as you are.'

Vera got out of Margaret's car, saying, 'I'll let you know. By the way I never really thanked you for recovering my car.'

'It recovered itself, Vera, there was nothing really wrong with it. And I hope the same applies to Geoff.'

'So do I!' Vera said sincerely as she closed the car door and walked over to her own Morris Minor. As she waved Margaret goodbye, she recollected Margaret liked Geoff. Was she imagining it — all of a sudden a fear gripped her heart — was Geoff having a secret affair with Margaret?

Margaret was unmarried, yet Geoff had helped her when she became pregnant and widowed within a short space of time. It had been long before Vera had met him, but had Margaret harboured a love for him?

Yes, she was an old friend — a good friend of Geoff's — but was it more than that?

Vera sat in her car wondering about Geoff long after Margaret's car had left the school car park.

Then she shook herself. There was no sense in sitting and imagining all sorts of unpleasant things.

Starting the car engine Vera decided she would have to find out the truth.

It was not possible to question Geoff until the boys were tucked up in bed for the night.

The spring weather was making the evenings lighter and after Vera had prepared supper for them both, the washing up had been done and the dogs taken out, they went to the sitting-room.

'I must talk to you seriously,' Vera said, taking out her knitting as that was one way she could save money by making the boys' jerseys.

Geoff was hidden behind the newspaper he was reading. He lowered it to say to his wife, 'What's the matter?'

'You.'

Geoff frowned.

'Don't look so surprised, Geoff.

You've been keeping me in the dark for long enough. Out with it!'

Geoff gave a sigh and shifted in his chair. 'I don't want you to worry.'

'That's ridiculous! How can I ignore you prowling about at night — and you look as if you are carrying a sandbag around with you. You are a very handsome man and I wondered if you were having an affair?'

Geoff looked at her keenly and, slowly putting down the crackly newspaper, he came and stood in front of her. 'Vera, I'm amazed. How can you say that? Or don't you love me anymore?'

Vera was relieved that unfaithfulness to his wife was not the issue, and she breathed more easily. 'Sorry, Geoff.' She put down her knitting and rose to give him a hug.

They stood and held each other tightly, kissing, until Geoff said, 'Perhaps it was wrong of me not to tell you, but I honestly thought it was better for me to keep my worries to myself.'

'How could you think that I wouldn't

notice you are troubled about something?'

Geoff gave a short laugh. He scratched the back of his neck saying, 'It's difficult for me to explain.'

She gasped. 'Are you unwell, suffering from something?'

He held her hands. 'Yes, I suppose you can say I'm a little uneasy . . . '

'Geoff, please stop beating about the bush and say exactly what is amiss. I must know.'

He led her to the sofa so that they could both sit together. 'My problem is simply that young Dickie Brightman is trying to push me out of my job — which is going to be changed very soon. The river authorities are reviewing the organisation after the floods — which is understandable as they must try and prevent any future disasters.'

Vera nodded. That made sense to her.

Geoff continued. 'The new job will mean more responsibilities, engineering and designing of preventative measures to combat the particular problems of the low-lying Fenlands. I'd be going over to the Netherlands to discuss their systems, as part of their land is under sea level, too.'

'I would have thought that kind of work would suit you,' remarked Vera.

'Oh, it does, and I'm well qualified and suited to the work, but that rat, Dickie Brightman, is determined to get rid of me.'

The mention of a rat, which he had good reason to loath, made Vera gasp. 'But I thought you liked him?'

'It's true, he was friendly when I first came here.'

'And he offered you accommodation during the floods, didn't he?'

'Yes, he did, although I never stayed there.'

Vera frowned, puzzled. 'So why?'

Geoff turned away and paced about the room, striking the furniture with his fist as he walked. 'He's claiming that I'm not the best candidate for the job.'

'But Geoff, your river banks held during the flood, surely that proves your ability to do the job?'

'He claims the credit for that, Vera.'

'How can he? I know you worked hard to protect them. You have the engineering knowledge. He was only helping you to get to know the area.'

Geoff gave a shrug. 'He says I was ill, absent during the worst part of the floods. I abandoned my post because of illness, and he was left in charge.'

Vera began to understand how a clever, ambitious engineer could try and usurp his boss. The reward would be great for any young engineer if he was promoted. And because Brightman had befriended Geoff when the older man was appointed, just before the floods began, it was easy for him to claim a lot of what Geoff had done was his work.

'Dickie Brightman is accusing me of being in hospital when I should have been at work.'

'That's hardly your fault that you worked all hours for weeks, just as I did, and became exhausted.'

Geoff raised his hands in a hopeless gesture. 'The chaps on the appointment boards are hard-nosed men, Vera. They will listen to Dickie as well as to me. They have to decide who they think would be best for the top job — and he knows the influential people here. Having been away in the Army, I don't know anyone who will back me.'

Geoff didn't say it, but Vera knew his pride was hurt. He must know he would be the best and experienced engineer for the work, and he needed the additional salary to pay for the huge debt on the house. But when an upstart wormed his way in, persuading influential people to back him, there was little Geoff could do because he had only recently come into the job and didn't know anyone like Brightman did to bat for him.

What would happen if Geoff lost his job?

Vera could see that their beautiful home would have to go on the market because she didn't earn enough with her Assistant Organiser job to pay the household bills as well as the mortgage.

'Oh, Geoff!' Vera cried. 'What will become of us?'

'Wait and see,' Geoff said, coming to her and wrapping his arms around her. 'The worst hasn't happened yet. The appointments are not going to be made until next month. In the meantime I'll carry on. I'm designing a new sluice gate — and may have that finished to show at the interview.'

'But those men at the interview won't know how clever your design is.'

'True, but they will like the way it will work — if I show them it does the job.'

Vera felt she was wound up as tight as a violin string, but she had to support Geoff who she now understood was in trouble. Whatever happened to his job she could always go and stay with her mother.

She looked at the clock on the mantelshelf. 'We must go to bed, dear, it's late. Thank you for telling me about your worry and I'm very sorry about it. You don't deserve that slap in the face — after serving your country during the war and working so hard at your new job. I want you to know that whatever happens to your job, it won't be the end of the world for us. We have each other, and our boys, a loving family — and at present, at least, a beautiful house to live in, too.'

She said no more as Geoff had pressed her close in his arms to stroke her hair and kiss her — and she was thankful that there was nothing to split them up. For better or for worse they were married, and as the worst had descended on them, they needed to comfort each other.

Bitter Words

Vera didn't tell Geoff she was going to Norwich to see Margaret.

The next day, she went towards her office in the early morning hoping Margaret hadn't gone out somewhere.

It was awesome entering the grand City Hall building. The receptionist told her where to go and soon she was standing outside a door marked, impressively with the notice, *School Meals Organiser, Miss Margaret Smallwood*, on the door.

She was about to knock when she heard a voice behind her, 'Miss Smallwood is out.'

Swinging around Vera saw a small, bespectacled man, carrying a sheaf of papers.

Vera's look of dismay must have prompted him to enquire, 'Can I help you?'

'Well, er, thank you. I really need to see Miss Smallwood.'

'I expect I can assist you — I know about her work.'

Vera didn't think he looked as if he was more than a clerk, but she said, 'I haven't come to see her about work . . . it's a private matter.'

The man who was about as tall as she was, blinked at her. Vera gulped, realising that by saying she'd come to pass the time of a working day chatting wasn't exactly wise. 'I mean, I'm one of her School Meal Organisers,' she said hurriedly.

His thick glasses shone and Vera thought she might be told to leave. She went on to explain quickly, 'My name is Vera Parkington, and I'm the organiser for the Fen district.'

'Come with me, if you will,' he said, marching off and she had no option but to follow him.

Was he showing her out of the building?

But he stopped walking and opened

an office door and indicated she should go in.

The office was empty. He pointed to a chair. She sat down while he went around the big desk and sat opposite her. Putting his papers down on the desk tidily, he looked at Vera and said, 'I'm sure you wouldn't have come from the other side of the county for a minor matter, Mrs Parkington.'

'Well, no. But before you think I've blown up an oven or come to ask her for time off, I assure you it is much more ... well, it's to do with my husband's job.'

She hadn't meant to mention what she'd come about to this insignificant little man, but she blurted it out, because it was on her mind.

He didn't react more that to give her a twisted smile. Then he said, 'Mrs Parkington, I've heard about your work during the floods, and if I can do something to help you — or your husband, I would be only too pleased.'

Amazed he'd heard about her, Vera's

heart began to pound.

What kind of a reputation had she got that it had found its way to the City Hall? What had Margaret been saying about her?

'I doubt if you could help,' she began. Then she gave a chuckle. 'It's to do with the River Authority — nothing like kitchen work.'

He blinked at her again. 'Whatever it may be, is it interfering with your work.'

Vera blushed. 'I suppose it is.'

'So tell me about it.'

There was something about that clerk which made Vera pour out her husband's troubles to him. He sat there like a gnome taking it all in nodding at times. When Vera had put all Geoff's difficulties before him he got up and Vera did, too, saying, 'Well, thank you for listening to my tale of woe. I was going to ask Miss Smallwood if she knew anyone who would help Geoff.'

'Miss Smallwood would have come to me,' he said, picking up his papers, 'I'm the Head of the Council.'

Vera's mouth fell open in surprise. 'I'd better get back to work,' she said, picking up her handbag, 'or you'll give me the sack.'

But he held out his hand to shake hers, saying, 'I'm pleased to have met you, Mrs Parkington. Although I know little about the River Authority's work — I know some of the men who work there. It's only right that your husband has the support he needs. But, of course, it will be for the panel of experts at the interview to make the decision on who gets the job.'

'I understand. But just knowing that Geoff — I mean, my husband, will have some people on his side — I mean who understand how skilled, and dedicated to the work he has been — it's a great relief.'

'Good work is never forgotten, Mrs Parkington. I'll tell Miss Smallwood you came, but I'll leave it to you to tell her what you've told me.'

After he'd opened the door and seen her out, he trotted off down the corridor before she could say more than, 'Thank you, sir.'

Vera didn't think that there was any point in hanging around to see Margaret and drove back to Ely pleased that her journey had not been in vain.

★　★　★

Horrid second thoughts crossed Vera's mind later.

Had she done the wrong thing by interfering in Geoff's affairs? Was the Head of the Council as sympathetic as he seemed to have been?

She had difficulty in concentrating on her work, and lost her temper when Peter started to toddle about and hide, just when she was trying to get the evening meal ready.

Plonking the child in his high chair she put his bowl of food before him and was furious when he began to throw it out of his dish and on to the floor, where the dogs snapped it up.

Vic thought it was funny and laughed

as he threw a piece of potato at Peter.

Vera shouted at the boys, 'Stop it at once! It's not funny to waste food. You know how difficult it is to feed everyone these days.'

She breathed loudly, feeling like a dragon. She'd spent the day trying to think of meals for school children using very little ingredients. She glared at her naughty boys saying, 'Neither of you will get any chocolate tonight!'

The smiles disappeared from the children's faces and the dogs slinked away to their baskets.

Immediately Vera felt guilty. Normally she would not have become so angry and would not have shouted at the children, telling them that food was scarce and they must eat it properly.

With tears in her eyes she turned towards the stove to get on with Geoff's meal.

Suddenly she felt a heavy hand on her shoulder. 'After the meal, you sit down,' said Geoff, 'I'll put the boys to bed when they've finished eating.'

Sniffing, Vera wiped her eyes with her hankie and replied, 'Thanks, I've had a terrible day — but so have you, I'm sure. I'm ever so sorry.'

Geoff was good with the children, who were less inclined to get up to mischief when their father was in charge of them.

Coming through in their pyjamas to say goodnight, Vic and Peter, prompted by Geoff, said they was sorry for their bad behaviour, but as Vera kissed them, she felt guilty about her own fit of temper.

'It's understandable you were cross with them,' Geoff told her later. 'We are both under strain at present. Our boys have to be taught they can't always do just as they like — they didn't get their sweet ration this evening — it won't hurt them, Vera.'

Vera didn't tell Geoff she'd been to the City Hall or that she'd made an effort to improve his application to be the Chief Engineer. There was no point in raising his hopes when she had no proof that her effort to help him would succeed.

As the days passed Vera began to realise why Geoff had been reluctant to tell her about the insecurity of his job. He had obviously wanted to avoid upsetting her — at least before it was necessary to do so.

Carrying the knowledge that she might lose her beautiful home and have to live on even less money than they had to at present, was daunting. Lying awake for hours, worrying about their future, she was sharing Geoff's burden — but was it just making her short tempered? Causing trouble between them?

When Geoff told her he had to go away on a course, Vera was suspicious.

'Why?' she asked. She was clearing up after their evening meal and her working day had seemed long. 'Can't you go to the meetings from here every day?'

Geoff, was becoming just as short tempered. 'No, I can't. The meetings are being held in London.'

She scrubbed at a dirty pan, saying testily, 'Why has it to be there — it's far away from your river?'

He sat at the kitchen table and rested his elbows on it, burying his face in his hands. 'Because,' he replied in a muffled voice, 'Our river was not the only one which flooded. Many rivers in England flooded and the authorities must try and prevent the disaster happening again, as far as they can. During the war years it was under-standable many flood defences were neglected, but now they must do something about it — design new barriers and the like.'

That to Vera sounded sensible. But she didn't like the idea of having to cope with two young children, her job and the housework on her own, and said so.

Geoff clearly lost his temper. 'How do you think housewives with children managed during the war while their men folk were away fighting?'

'The war is over,' Vera said feebly. 'And I would like to know why things are getting more difficult instead of getting better?'

Her husband stood scraping back his chair said, 'I'd better go and pack.'

Vera, who was facing the sink sighed loudly and said, 'Go on then.'

But Geoff had already stamped out of the room.

Aghast that she'd caused him to become angry, and that it was clearly her fault, she felt the tears come into her eyes.

She went to sit on the chair he'd vacated. Staring miserably into space. Feeling a failure.

After waiting a while for him to return, which he didn't, she decided it was necessary for her to apologise and, getting up, she went to look for him.

She looked upstairs. The boys were sleeping peacefully in their bedrooms. He wasn't in their bedrooms. He wasn't in their bedroom. He must be down-stairs.

Descending the staircase she thought she heard a noise outside the house. Going to the landing window, which looked out over the front of the house, she saw Geoff's car slowly moving away from the house and down the road.

Sitting on the staircase, Vera sobbed as she realised he'd already taken a few of his things — and left her!

Unexpected News

It was only after Vera had cleared up the kitchen, somewhat in a daze, and fed the dogs and letting them out, she crept up to bed. Lying down in the dark, feeling drained of strength and more unhappy than she'd felt in her life, she felt something on her pillow.

Switching on her bedside light she saw it was a note. With her sight swimming with tears she feared to read it for some minutes.

Dearest Vera,
    I feel I can't avoid hurting you if I stay at home.
    Manage as best you can.
    Love, Geoff.

The note was scribbled hurriedly She held it to her breast. He'd written, *love, Geoff.* Or did it mean goodbye?

She cried some more, until exhaustion overtook her and she slept fully clothed.

When morning came she was woken up by the dogs barking, the black cloud of misery descended on her, but also the need to rush downstairs to see the dogs waiting for their early morning walk and Vic standing on a kitchen stair, stretching to reach the cornflakes, which fell out of the cupboard as he tried to grasp it.

'Mum, I'm sorry,' the little boy said, looking down at the cornflakes spilled over the kitchen floor. Soon not only the dogs, but Pete was picking them up and eating them.

Vera could tell that they were not misbehaving — it was late, and she should have been there earlier to get the children's breakfast. Taking a huge breath, she picked up the packet of cereal, saying, 'Sit down and I'll get your bowls out.'

Vera laid the bowls out on the table and filled them with the cornflakes from the packet, and put some milk and sugar over them.

She swept Pete into his high chair, and let the dogs eat the rest of the cornflakes on the floor — it saved her from having to sweep them up.

'Where's Dad?' asked Vic as he finished munching his cornflakes.

Vera, who'd made herself a cup of tea, steadied her hand as she put her cup down on her saucer slowly. She took a deep breath. 'He had to rush away last night,' she replied. Then she added, 'He may be away for some time.'

'Where's he gone?'

Vera wondered. He wouldn't have gone to stay with Dickie Brightman, who'd offered him accommodation before — or his family who lived miles away. He may have gone to London to stay with a friend . . . perhaps, despite him denying it, he had a girlfriend somewhere — he was a very handsome man.

She hadn't long to think about it, though, as her son repeated the question. 'Mum, where's Dad gone?'

'He had to go to London.'

'Can we go there?'

'You will. One day. Now go and get ready for school.'

Having been punished the previous day for bad behaviour, Vic seemed determined to co-operate, which made things easier for Vera. She had to take Pete over to his baby-sitter, Vic to school, and the dogs for a short run before she started work. There wasn't much time left to consider whether or not her beloved Geoff was being unfaithful.

What if he was? There was nothing she could do about it anyway. Best not to dwell on thinking the worst of him.

He could be lying low, as his note suggested, on his own to cope with the traumatic changes that were about to happen to his job. Suppose his junior, Dickie Brightman, did overtake him and he had to work under him? Vera herself had had that happen to her when Margaret became her boss, and as it happened the transfer had suited her. Vera knew she wouldn't want Margaret's job at present. It would be too much for her with two children to bring up.

The days without Geoff seemed long, tiring, and dull and she hated being on her own in the evenings.

When her mother rang Vera tried to sound more cheerful that she felt.

'You sound a little flat, Vera.'

'After a busy day, I feel it. I've just put the boys to bed.'

'I thought Geoff helped you by reading the bedtime stories.'

'Well, yes, normally he does. But he's very busy at work at the moment.'

There was a pause then her mother said, 'He isn't with you, is he?'

How did her mother know that? Vera's head was in a spin. At first she didn't know what to say. 'No,' she said carefully. 'There's a big reorganisation going on after the floods, so he's working on that at the moment and staying there.'

'Where?'

Vera felt exasperated. 'Mum, I don't know. Somewhere in London. In some hotel I should think. He left in a hurry last night.'

'It's not like Geoff to rush off like that without telling you where he's going.'

There was no fooling her mother, so Vera had to tell the truth. Having all the facts straight, Mum told her she was coming over to help her.

'I can manage, Mum,' Vera said. 'Honestly.'

'It's not just a case of managing,' Alice said, 'I can tell you are *uptight,* as the youngsters say these days. You need someone to walk the dogs for you and help with the children.'

'There's nowhere for you to sleep'

But her mother was not going to be put off. 'Victor can sleep in his brother's room on our camp bed that we'll bring. You can sleep in Victor's bed and we'll sleep in your double bed.'

'Victor won't like that!'

'Vera! You must bring your son up to be flexible. Learn to put up with things if necessary at times.'

Vera bristled, 'Poor little Vic has had to put up with a lot of things since the floods began. He's been very good and helpful. He even had his Penguin destroyed!'

'Did he? Poor little chap. I never knew when I knitted him that toy it would become his favourite.'

'Isobel gave him a red Dinky toy car. He likes that.'

'Have you heard how Len and Isobel are faring?'

'They have rung a couple of times. They seem to be doing well.'

Vera thought that by chatting to her mother about Isobel, she might forget her plan to come over to Ely. But no, she was told firmly to expect them tomorrow. 'And I'll bring sheets — so you won't have to worry about washing them.'

So that was it. Vera accepted she'd inherited her mother's stubborn nature. Mum and her step-father were coming to stay — whether she liked it or not.

Of course, deep in her heart, she was grateful. They would be a great help and comfort.

⋆   ⋆   ⋆

'If the worst happens,' said Alice to her daughter as they were taking a stroll in the park with Pete in his push chair, 'and Geoff loses his job in the re-organisation, he can always get another job.'

Vera retorted, 'It's not that easy. There are still millions of ex-servicemen trying to find their feet after the war. Some of them had specialist jobs in the Army, Navy or Air Force.'

'Ah, but Geoff is an engineer.'

'Mum, Geoff needs a job that will interest him.'

Alice looked at her daughter sceptically. 'He may have to start at the bottom, but his ability will help him to rise quickly.'

Vera huffed. 'He has done that

already. But now he is being pushed out — '

'You don't know that for sure yet, Vera! You really must stop thinking that all changes are going to hurt you.'

Vera said no more. Her mother was well meaning but she didn't fully understand how fearful she was of the future ahead of her. She'd been through a lot of upheaval recently with the floods. It wasn't just her future she worried about.

Geoff had overcome his emotional illness and she didn't want him knocked down again. Vic was happy at his school and she had a safe job.

Now all that may change. She would have to start all over again and she felt strangely tired. She'd a nice house — which they were in danger of losing if they couldn't afford it. The thought of having to go back to that rat-infested cottage appalled her.

'I suspect you are not entirely well,' her mother went on while Vera was contemplating.

'What do you mean? There's nothing wrong with me, Mum. I'm just a bit worried, that's all. I dare say you are right that we will overcome our difficulties — but just at present . . . '

It was awful to find herself bathed in tears as she walked along. Afraid to turn her head and face her mother.

'I'm going to insist you go to see your doctor.'

'We haven't one.'

'Vera!' Her mother stopped walking and stamped her foot. 'The new National Health Service has been in operation for ages, you should have done something about it.'

'I've been far too busy. Anyway, Geoff reads the newspapers and listens to the radio. He should have told me about it.'

Her mother huffed looking at her distraught daughter. 'I came here to help you, and I can see you need some assistance in that direction. We'll go to your local surgery today and sign you and your family on to the National

Health list — and get an appointment for you to see your new doctor.'

'I don't need a doctor. He can't do anything about my heartache.'

'It may not be that.'

Vera snorted. 'I can always go to the chemist for a bottle of tonic, but I don't believe that does any good. Good food is the answer.' Vera wiped her tears with her hankie. 'Wartime rations are beginning to end at last . . . bread is whiter than it was during the war years. Do you know I saw some bananas on sale the other day when I was shopping? Of course, most of the extra food is too expensive for us to buy, but isn't it wonderful to see things for sale we haven't seen for years?'

'Ducks!' shouted Pete excitedly from his pushchair.

Vera was reminded that they had come to see ducks. Soon they would have enough bread left over for her little son to feed them. He'd love that.

Vera's mother insisted she went to see her new National Health doctor, and Vera accepted a check up might not be a bad idea.

She never dreamed she would be pregnant!

'That's the last thing I wanted!' she told the doctor crossly. 'As if I hadn't enough troubles already.'

He doctor ignored her grumbles. 'You're a healthy woman, Mrs Parkington, and another child shouldn't give you any trouble.'

'It will,' Vera said. Although she was secretly pleased, an additional member of the family would mean . . . lots of adjustments.

'The National Health allows you extra food and you will receive free medical care.'

When she got home she wished Geoff was there to tell him, but her mother and step-father were delighted with the news.

'You knew I was pregnant, didn't you, Mum?'

'I suspected it,' said Alice with a nod.

Vera kissed her mother. 'To tell the

truth I feel much better now I know why I was becoming so tired. I have to go to the maternity clinic and he said I would receive free medical care — it all seems too good to be true.'

Her mother and step-father looked at each other and smiled.

★ ★ ★

Miles away in London, Geoffrey Parkington was being questioned about his suitability for the job of Chief Engineer. As an ex-colonel in the Royal Engineers, he was smartly dressed, and demonstrated his skill by answering their civil engineering questions easily.

He impressed the interview board with newly acquired knowledge of river maintenance. That and the fact that the river banks he was in charge of held — even after the worst floods the Fens had ever known.

But were his nerves stable enough to take on the responsibility of the increased size of the job?

The other main candidate they were considering claimed Mr Parkington was not stable. He had become ill and unable to continue working at the height of the disaster.

'Is Mr Brightman merely putting the other candidate down to secure the job himself?' one interviewer put the question to the others.

The board was divided. Some claimed the older, more experienced man, who had served his country well during the war, deserved the job. While others seemed to think the younger man, who had spent years working for the River Board, was the better man for the job.

It was tense in the waiting-room. While Geoff sat trying to remain cool, and polite, his rival, Dickie Brightman paced the room, seeming to suggest he thought he shouldn't be kept waiting because he was clearly the man they should select for the job.

'If I'm not given the job,' Dickie blurted out, 'I'll go to another River Authority.'

Geoff refrained from saying anything other than, 'Well, good luck to you.'

But Geoff, despite his military training, felt his heart thump with nervousness. When at last the door of the interview room opened. A man came out and turning to Mr Parkington, he asked him to come into the interview room again.

Geoff rose to his feet and without glancing at his opponent, followed the man into the interview room. There was no telling whether they were going to offer him the job — or if they wanted to see him to explain why they had given the job to the other candidate.

Life Goes On

'I just don't know how I could have managed without you and John, Mum,' Vera said, kissing her mother as she sat down for the breakfast her mother had prepared for her.

'We all need help at times,' Alice said, putting a boiled egg in the egg cup on Vera's plate. As an expectant mother, Vera was allowed extra food rations and the additional food and rest she was getting was making her feel much better.

'I'll have to tell Margaret I'm pregnant,' Vera said. 'I don't know how she'll manage without me — or how we'll manage for that matter.'

He mother poured a cup of tea for Vera and herself and brought them to the table saying, 'What day will Geoff know about his job?'

'I don't know,' Vera said cracking the

egg and carefully taking off the top. 'If he doesn't get the chief's job we will be hard pressed to live for a while until I can get back to work.'

'Did Isobel and Len stipulate how they wanted to be paid for the house?'

Vera sat with her spoon poised to start eating. 'Not that I know of.'

'Well then, don't worry about it. From what you tell me they are sensible people. They have a new place to live in Scotland and while your family are young they won't expect you to be able to give them much.'

'If anything,' remarked Vera, popping some of the creamy yellow egg into her mouth.

He mother took a sip of tea. 'You should hear from Geoff any day now, dear.'

'Mum, I fear he might be so disappointed, about not getting the job, he might — well he could do anything . . . '

'Don't talk like that, Vera. You are trying to jump fences before it is necessary. Whatever the result, you will survive. Heavens, you both survived D-Day in France!'

'Geoff has battle scars.'

'It didn't prevent him from getting up on his feet again. Can't you see you have a lot going for you? My goodness, Vera, many a man would give up a good job just to have a loving family as you have.'

Vera smiled. 'Of course you are right, Mum.' She finished eating her egg in silence. Then she said, 'Where is everyone?'

'John has taken Vic to school, with the dogs on leads and I am going out shopping with Pete in the pushchair. I thought we'd have cauliflower cheese for lunch — will that suit you?'

'I'll take the vacuum round and dust a bit.'

'Well don't carry the heavy vacuum upstairs. Wait for John to come back and carry it up for you.'

'Yes, Mother,' said Vera with a grin.

Her mother was putting on her hat.

She never went out to town without a hat and gloves — it was considered necessary by older women to be properly dressed. Although Vera could feel a new air of change in society now the war was over. Many things, like hats and gloves, were beginning to be thought unnecessary.

Alone in the house, vacuuming the carpet, Vera thought about what her mother had said. Yes, she still hoped that whatever happened to Geoff they would be able to stay in this house — which she now felt was her own.

With the noise of the sweeper she didn't hear her mother leave the house, or Geoff's car swinging into the drive.

She didn't even hear him come in the front door and stand watching her as she sang a little to herself as she swept the carpet.

Suddenly she was aware of his presence.

'Geoff!'

He said nothing but came to take her in his arms. 'Oh, Geoff,' she said, too overcome to say anything else.

And he didn't say anything, either. He just held her and kissed her tenderly.

All was right between them and that was all that really mattered.

Vera hadn't told her mother exactly how they had parted and the dreadful ache she had that he might not come back. Now she was glad she hadn't said anything as it was obvious that there was no rift between them. They were as one as they always had been.

'Would you like a cup of tea?' she asked him.

Vera slipped from his arms and went into the kitchen while he raced upstairs to put the things from his bag away. She felt as if she was in a dream. There were so many things she wanted to know, but she couldn't think of any.

Geoff had come home safe and sound and that was all that really mattered.

Coming downstairs a little later, he said, 'I see your mum and step-father are here.'

'Yes, they came to help me out.'

'It wasn't fair of me to leave you, I'm sorry.'

Vera replied robustly, 'I wasn't making things easy for you at a critical time in your life — by the way, what happened about your job?'

'What do you think — the best man got it.'

Vera laughed. 'Well done!' She couldn't say she always knew he would — the whole waiting period had given her nightmares. Nether did she like to admit she hadn't always thought he would be successful.

But relief flooded over her. Vera couldn't help her eyes from dancing — her arms from reaching out for his.

'I have some news for you, too,' she whispered.

★ ★ ★

Having to consider an additional member of the family was Vera's next challenge.

Before Alice and John went home

they told Geoff and Vera how pleased they were to have been able to help over the past few weeks — and they were thanked for their kindly assistance.

'You've been wonderful.' Vera kissed her mother and her step-father as they decided to leave as soon as they knew Geoff was back.

'That's what grandparents are for,' replied Alice, who Vera thought looked tired after hectic few days with her.

'How fortunate I am to have my mother!' Vera sighed seeing her go.

A new life awaited her once more.

Geoff had his job, with the added responsibility of being the top man. Vera was anxious at first that he would manage and it was soon apparent that he was well suited to the work.

Only she couldn't help feeling a little jealous that his career was thriving while she was stuck in a backwater as far as hers was concerned. Being a simple cook was not her ambition and as the food rationing was gradually easing after the war, she wanted to experiment with more high-class cookery.

She told herself that she should be content with bringing up her family and having a job she could do without too much difficulty.

Not mentioning her dissatisfaction to Geoff, or her mother, she blurted out the problem to Margaret when they next met.

They had gone to a warehouse to examine some of the new kitchen equipment that school kitchens were going to be issued with.

Margaret explained, 'There will be no more cooked meals being made in a central kitchen, then put into canisters to be carted out to small schools. Each school is to have a fully equipped kitchen on site and, as some of the older schools are being rebuilt in the future, brand-new kitchens need to be designed.'

'Just your cup of tea,' Vera said, knowing Margaret to be an excellent organiser.

'Yes,' Margaret agreed.

Vera knew Margaret was not only competent, but very confident — which made Vera feel the opposite.

'That brings me to another change . . .' Margaret continued.

Vera wouldn't have been surprised if her friend had said she was intending to become Prime Minister! After the war women had certainly begun to take over jobs that used to be for men only.

'It will affect you.'

Vera quaked. Was Margaret going to suggest that, as she was with child, she gave up work?

'Your job is going to disappear.'

'Disappear?' Vera said. Although quietly she'd thought for some time that she was superfluous. The school meal cooks in her area were good and didn't need her going around to make sure of the fact.

'Never fear, I have another job for you!'

'What do you intend to do with your left-over supervisors?'

'Well, I have a special job lined up for you, Vera. Don't look so worried, it is one I think you will like. I'll tell you more about it on Saturday. May I come around for coffee at about eleven?'

Intrigued, Vera enquired if it was to do with cooking.

'Of course it is!'

Margaret seemed to be more interested in inspecting the huge refrigerators and was not intending to tell her anything more at present, so Vera had to try and concentrate on the refrigerators, too. It wasn't too difficult because the latest kitchen equipment, all shiny and new, fascinated her as well as Margaret.

Vera could appreciate that cooking skills could be enhanced by the latest inventions and gadgets coming on to the market. There were to be many changes coming in the future.

Saturday seemed a long time coming and when it did Geoff sensed Vera was a little jumpy. 'What's up?' he asked as he picked up the hair brush she had dropped on the bedroom floor.

'Margaret is coming around to tell me about the new job she thinks I might like.'

Geoff immediately sympathised with her concern. 'I'll take the boys out to the park while she's here, Vera. Then you and Margaret can have a good chat. Just remember you can't work for a while anyway, with the baby due. Anyway, if you don't like the sound of what she offers you, you don't have to take it. I earn enough to get us by.'

'But we will pay off our debt quicker if I do.'

'True, but it is the quality of our lives that matters. While the children are young you want to have the time to enjoy them.'

Vera finished putting on her lipstick and smiled at Geoff. 'You're right, of course. I know how tired I've been in the past when having too much to do. I'll hear what Margaret says and then we can decide.'

Vera was delighted when Margaret turned up with her small daughter,

Deanna. The little girl had her mother's confidence, peachy skin and curls around her lively face. How pretty the little girl was, and Vera secretly envied Margaret having a daughter.

While the children played together, with Geoff keeping an eye on them, Vera made some coffee then the women sat together and chatted.

'Now what about the job you had in mind for me?' asked Vera.

Margaret helped herself to a peanut butter biscuit Vera had made, crunched it, and remarked how delicious they were. Then she said, 'There's a grand hotel I know needing a specialist chef for their banquets and special occasions, like weddings. It's not a full-time job, but is well paid. It will mean working some weekends. The kitchens are well equipped, and the kitchen and dining-room staff are first class. It's not far for you to travel. And when you leave your present job, you'll be allowed to buy your car.'

'That'll suit me perfectly,' Vera said

smiling broadly.

'I can see it will mean I'll be working some weekends, too,' said Geoff, over-hearing the description of Vera's new job as he came strolling into the room for his cup of coffee.

'It won't kill you!' retorted Margaret. 'You have got your dream job, so you must let Vera have hers.'

Geoff gave both women a kiss. 'I wouldn't dare disagree,' he said, laughing.

Their daughter was born later that year. Vera was overjoyed to have her, but what name to give the child was a bit of a problem.

'Alice, after my mum? Or, Jane, after your mum? Or Isobel — after she so kindly arranged for us to buy her house?' mused Vera, nursing the infant.

'Well what about me having a say in the matter?' asked Geoff.

Vera looked up and smiled at him.

'The boys and I have already named her.'

Vera looked at him quizzically. 'Go on, tell me.'

'Cathy — Catherine.'

Vera thought about the name for a few moments, then said, 'Why not? It's a nice name. And if you and the boys like it, too — that's fine by me.'

THE END